GW00360042

Past-into-Present Series

THE THEATRE

Peter Lane

B T BATSFORD LTD London & Sydney

First published 1975

ISBN 0 7134 2952 6

Printed by The Anchor Press, Tiptree
for the Publishers B T Batsford Ltd
4 Fitzhardinge Street London W1H OAH
23 Cross Street Brookvale NSW 2100 Australia

For Clare Veronica

Acknowledgment

The Author and Publishers would like to thank the following for their kind permission to reproduce copyright illustrations: *The Daily Telegraph* for fig 1; the British Tourist Authority for fig 2; the National Tourist Organization of Greece for figs 3, 4, 5; the French Tourist Office for fig 6; Raymond Mander and Joe Mitchenson Theatre Collection for figs 7, 9, 11, 12, 14, 17, 19, 22, 30, 31, 36-43, 45-58, 63; the National Museum of Wales for fig 8; the Mansell Collection for figs 10, 13, 15, 23, 27, 28, 29; Keystone Press Agency for fig 16; Guildhall Art Gallery for figs 18, 24; National Portrait Gallery for figs 20, 25, 32; the Governors, Dulwich College, for fig 21; the Trustees of the Chatsworth Settlement for figs 34, 35; the Tate Gallery, London, for fig 44; Fox Photos for figs 59, 60; Times Newspapers for fig 61; the Mermaid Theatre for fig 62. Other illustrations appearing in this book are the property of the Publishers.

Contents

The Illustrations

Chapter 1. The Relevance of the Theatre

The illustration below is from the advertisement columns of a daily newspaper. You can see from this that there are a number of different plays and shows being put on at various London theatres. If you look at the advertisement columns of your local newspaper, you will see that there are many shows being presented in your district too. In some places touring companies will be putting on a play before or after its appearance at a London theatre. In other towns the local professional theatrical company will be staging its weekly show – perhaps a

1 Some of the plays and shows on in London, 1974.

APOLLO. 437 2663. Eve. 8.0. Mats. Thurs. 3. Sats. 6.0, 8.30.
DEREK NIMMO
"SUPERCLOWN," D. Express.
KATY MANNING
WHY NOT STAY FOR BREAKFAST?
"Derek Nimmo is gentle, tender, very, very funny and extremely touching. Both play and performances are to be warmly recommended," Harold Hobson, Sunday Times.

CAMBRIDGE. 836 6056. Mon. to Thurs. 8.0. Fri. & Sats. 5.45 & 8.30
Sixth Laughter Month of
PATRICK CARGILL
in London's new comedy Smash hit
TWO AND TWO MAKE SEX
"A HILARIOUS ROMP." People.

COMEDY. 930 2578. Evgs. 8.0. Mat. Th. 3.0. Sat. 5.30. 8.30
PAULINE COLLINS in JUDIES JOHN ALDERTON
"FILLS THE GLOOM OF LONDON WITH HIGH VOLTAGE LAUGHTER," SUN.

CRITERION. 930 3216. Eves. 8. Wed. 3 Sat. 5.30 & 8.40. Richard BRIERS, Shelia HANCOCK, Anna CALDER MARSHALL, Michael ALDRIDGE, David BURKE, Bridget TURNER in Alan AYCKBOURN'S
ABSURD PERSON SINGULAR
"BEST COMEDY OF THE YEAR," EVENING STANDARD AWARD.

DUCHESS. 836 8243
Evgs. 8.0 Fri., Sat. 6.15, 9.0.
OH! CALCUTTA!
OVER 1,400 PERFORMANCES
BREATHTAKINGLY BEAUTIFUL ST
THE NUDITY IS STUNNING, D.T.

Use prefix 01 only when telephoning from OUTSIDE LONDON

HER MAJESTY'S. 930 6606.
Limited Season.
Previews Feb. 14, 15, 16, 18, 19 at 8.0. Opens Feb. 20 at 7.0
REX HARRISON
YVONNE MITCHELL
in PIRANDELLO'S
HENRY IV
with JAMES VILLIERS

HOWFF, 109a, Regent's Park Road. NW1. FREE WHISKY—Boo and hiss the villain in THE DRUNKARD at The Howff Theatre. The most intelligent remark from the preview audiences wins 5 cases of Scotch Whisky. Previews until Feb. 12 at 8 p.m. Res.: 586 0030.

KING'S ROAD THEATRE 352 7488 Mon.-Th. 9.0. Fri., Sat. 7.30, 9.30
THE ROCKY HORROR SHOW
Best musical of year ES Drama awards

LYRIC. 437 3686. Evenings 8.0. *Mat. Wed. 3.0. Sat. 5.00 8.30
ALEC GUINNESS in
HABEAS CORPUS
by ALAN BENNETT.
WARM THEATRE & GENERATOR.

MAY FAIR 629 3036. Evgs. 8.15 Sat. 5.0 & 8.15. Limited Season.
ROY DOTRICE in
BRIEF LIVES
"What a joy it is"—F. Times. "Delightful," Tel. "Brilliant" Ppl

MERMAID. 248 7656. Rest. 2835. Red. price prevs. Wed. Th. Fri. 8.15. Sat. 5.0 & 8.15. Opens Feb. 11 at 7.0 Subs. 8.15. Wed. & Sat. 5.0 & 8.15.
SOMETHING'S BURNING
A New Play by RONALD EYRE.

THEATRE ROYAL WINDSOR. 95 61107. From Tues: ROAR LIKE A DOVE by Leslie Storm.

THEATRE UPSTAIRS. 730 2554. Daily 2.30. TWO JELLIPLAYS by Anne Jellicoe. Suitable 4-11 yr olds

TH. WORKSHOP. Stratford. E.15. 534 0310. Evs. 8, Sat. 5 & 8.
GENTLEMEN PREFER ANYTHING

VAUDEVILLE. 836 9988. Evgs. 8. Mats. Tues. 2 45. Sat. 5 & 8.
"COCKIE"
A MUSICAL ON THE CAREER OF CHARLES B. COCHRAN
with the unforgettable music of Richard RODGERS, Noel COWARD, Cole PORTER, Irving BERLIN, Jerome KERN George GERSHWIN.
"This Max Wall, this sweet and lovely Max Wall is a genius," Obs.
"Avril Angers . . triumphs," F.Times

VICTORIA PALACE. 834 1317.
Twice nightly 6.15 & 8.45
CARRY ON LONDON
SIDNEY JAMES, BARBARA WINDSOR, KENNETH CONNOR, BERNARD BRESSLAW, JACK DOUGLAS, PETER BUTTERWORTH. Book Now!
"The fun is practically gilt edged." Sunday Times.
Now booking until June 29
Theatre fully heated.

WHITEHALL. 930 6692/7765. 5th yr. Evgs. 8.30. Wed Sat. 6.15, 8.45
PAUL RAYMOND'S
PYJAMA TOPS

WYNDHAM'S. 836 3028. Mon. to Thurs. at 8.15 Fri. Sat. 6.15 & 9.0
GODSPELL
"IS MAGNIFICENT." Sun. Times.

Shakespearean play, a Restoration comedy, or a modern play by an American, French, Italian or British playwright.

Many of you will have taken part in the production of your own school play, or may belong to an amateur company attached to a youth club, church, or similar organization. More of you may have 'Drama' as one of the subjects on the school timetable, while others may be using drama as a means of learning history, scripture or current affairs.

Those of you who have none of these advantages will know about drama and the theatre from your own life and that of younger brothers and sisters. I have just watched my own three-year-old son pretending to be a 'baddy' in a game he is playing with his older brothers. Their whole game is in fact a play, which they are acting out without any script or directors. They are producing their own play – and are not worried whether there is an audience or not.

It seems then that theatre and drama are things which even the youngest of us do for ourselves – playing at 'Cops and Robbers', 'Cowboys and Indians', or 'Mothers and Fathers'. Drama is also something which we study at school and take part in at school, and which intelligent grown-ups both want to do and watch.

What is 'Theatre'?

There are three answers to this question. Obviously the theatre is a building or place in which a show is presented. Then there is the play itself, without which there would be no need for the building. Finally, there is one particular presentation or production of the play in a certain place – with scenery, lighting, curtains, costumes and so on.

In this book we will trace the ways in which these three different 'theatres' have developed and are continuing to develop. We will see how the buildings have altered, how different sorts of plays were offered at different times and in different countries, and how the style of presentation has changed – and is still changing. We will see that each age and each country has its own particular theatre.

Chapter 2. The First Theatre - the Greeks

Primitive Man and the Theatre

We know very little about how primitive men lived – they left us no written records, letters, diaries or newspapers from which to get some idea of their way of life. However, we do know that they did much more than merely hunt animals for food and clothing. We know, for example, that they worshipped gods for whom they built some sort of temple and to whom they offered sacrifices. We know that even in their cave homes they liked to relive some of the exciting incidents in their lives. They have left us some very beautiful

2 Stonehenge – the scene of ancient religious ceremonies. The Druid priests were in many ways like leading actors, with the altar as their stage and the faithful as their audience.

drawings – of animals, people and their methods of hunting, for instance. We can imagine the cave artist talking as he went about his work – and being talked to by the others who were keen to remind him about this, that or the other incident or animal.

If these primitive people were anxious to express their feelings through drawings, it is also likely that they acted out some of these incidents; after all, it is a natural instinct to want to act – even the youngest children do it in their games. It is also natural that if men are trying to explain how they scored a goal or won a battle they use various actions, facial expressions and bodily movements, to help make the story more realistic.

Religion and Theatre

In every known civilization the first glimmerings of theatrical productions have been linked with religious rituals. In these, a group of priests or leaders was marked off from the others by their different costume. There were the processions of the priests, their attendants and the crowd to the temple. There were songs, dances and other rituals associated with whatever form of worship the people were attending. All these activities were, in many ways, dramatic and theatrical productions – with the priests as the star actors, the dancers as the supporting chorus and the crowd participating in a very real way. These religious rituals were attempts to arouse the emotions of people – by word and action – which is what drama sets out to achieve. Music, costume and scenery were used as they still are today as audio and visual aids, and in these early religious rituals we can see the beginnings not only of modern drama, but of ballet, opera, cinema and TV productions.

The Athenians and their Theatre

The real roots of modern theatre and drama, however, are to be found in Greece. Indeed, the word 'drama' comes from a Greek word *dran*, meaning to do. By 480 BC the city state of Athens was the leading Greek state, with a record of great victories over its neighbours and a successful and rich trading system. The Athenian citizens were wealthy enough to spare time and money for many intellectual pursuits. It was in Athens that Aristotle (384-322 BC) laid the foundations for modern politics. Another Athenian, Plato (427-347 BC), is the father of modern philosophy, and the state's architects and sculptors produced work which is still admired and copied today. It is not surprising that the Athenians also laid the foundations on which modern drama and theatre is built.

The Athenians believed that all citizens had the right to participate in every public happening, including theatrical productions. This explains the shape of their first theatres. These had to be places where thousands of men could gather to see a play, so the Athenians built them as large, open spaces,

3 The theatre at Delphi. The ruins of Apollo's Temple can be seen immediately behind the remains of the stage buildings. Notice how the Greeks used the natural slopes to provide seating for their audiences.

surrounded by sloping banks where men could either stand or sit and still see the production.

We have already noted that the earliest forms of dramatic presentation were linked with religious ritual. This was as true of Athens as of other civilizations. Thus the first Athenian theatres were near temples, and the first plays were representations of the myths and legends which every educated Athenian already knew.

Inside the Theatre

In time the Athenians improved on nature with its slopes and open spaces, and began to build their own theatres. Some of you may have visited the ruins of an ancient Athenian theatre. The theatre was still an open space, with sloping sides where men stood or sat to watch what was happening below, on the semi-circle which the Greeks called the orchestra. On this stood about 50 players who made up the most important part of the Greek dramatic society – the chorus. This chorus spoke the lines and performed the simple actions or mimes that made up the early plays.

Behind the orchestra was the stage and the buildings where the chorus changed their costumes and kept their stage properties, weapons, musical instruments and so on. In front of the orchestra were the best seats, where priests and other important officials sat. When dramatists later introduced individual actors into their plays, these appeared on the 'proscenium' in front of the 'skene' – from which we get our modern word scene, or scenery.

Actors and Playwrights

In the sixth century BC, a Greek called Thespis wrote plays in which he used a single actor to speak some of the lines, although the chorus still did most of the

work. This one actor was called a 'protagonist' – someone who spoke for (or 'pro') whatever was being discussed. This was a major step forward in the history of the theatre; for the first time we have an actor appearing on the stage. The importance of this development is recognized by the use of the word 'Thespian' to describe the art or profession of acting.

Thespis's actor played a variety of parts, using masks to show the audience that at one time he was speaking as person A and at another time as person B. The playwright Aeschylus (525-456 BC) introduced a second actor into his plays. Aeschylus wrote about 90 plays – of which only seven are now known. He has been called the 'father of Greek tragedy', largely because he was the first playwright to try to move away from plays about myths and legends, and to examine instead some of the real problems that affected ordinary people in their daily lives.

Another famous Greek dramatist was Sophocles (496-406 BC), who improved on Aeschylus's work by introducing a further two actors onto the stage. Sophocles was an expert musician before becoming a leading general in the Athenian army and later a dramatist. He was a fine example of the Greek ideal citizen – well-educated and capable of tackling a variety of tasks.

Sophocles reduced the part played by the chorus in his plays, and gave greater importance to the individual actors. We only have copies of 7 of the 123 plays which he wrote, but among these is his famous *Oedipus Rex*, which some of you may have seen on TV or at the theatre.

Euripides (484-407 BC) is in some ways the most important of the Greek dramatists. In his plays he gave parts to many actors, so diminishing even

4 (*Opposite*) Herod Atticus Theatre, Athens. In the centre, below the steeply tiered rows of seats, is the semi-circular orchestra, while in the background you can see the wooden stage and the theatre buildings.

5 (*Right*) A modern performance in an ancient theatre of *Oedipus Coloneus*, by Sophocles. This was one of the first plays in which individual actors were given prominence.

further the role of the chorus which had once dominated the theatre. He also enlarged the scope of the dramatist's work by emphasizing man's ordinary experiences and paying less attention to myths, legends and religion.

By doing this Euripides was reflecting in his work the new moral and social influences which were beginning to affect Athenian life. Like many of his contemporaries, he was sceptical about religion with its hundreds of gods. But most Athenians were more traditional than Euripides, and he was not well-liked. He became even more unpopular when he opposed a majority decision in favour of more war, a wider empire and greater military expenditure. In 408 BC he went into voluntary exile and died in the following year.

It is well to note that each of these three leading Greek dramatists built on the work of others. Aeschylus introduced one actor, Sophocles brought two onto the stage, while Euripides wrote parts for many. We should also notice that a dramatist's work represents the attitudes of his time. Because of this, each age has its own form of theatre. And when the attitudes and morals of the time are in a state of flux, then the work of dramatists will reflect these changes. Some people will write plays which present the ideas of the older, traditional, conservative members of their society. Others, like Euripides, will reflect the ideas of the younger, radical and rebellious groups, and thus come into conflict with the traditionalists who think that their work is immoral, blasphemous, irreligious and fit only to be banned. We have this struggle in our own time – with shows like *Oh Calcutta!* and *Hair* – as Euripides did in his. Nothing, it seems, changes very much.

Chapter 3. From the Roman Theatre to Miracle Plays

The Roman Theatre

As the power of the Greeks declined that of the Romans increased and, in time, Rome became the centre of the largest empire the world had ever known. As well as being a great military people, the Romans had very many expert architects and builders. Among the great buildings were the Roman theatres and amphitheatres which, unlike the Greek ones, were built on level ground with the seats arranged in sloping tiers on concrete foundations. Some of you may have seen their ruins in Italy; others may have visited the remains in Britain which date from the Roman occupation of the country during the first four centuries AD.

But if the Romans could build better theatres than the Greeks, they were unable to produce any great playwrights. Most of them – like Terence and Plautus – merely imitated the great Greek writers, and few of their plays are very significant. Others, such as Seneca, wrote plays which they wanted people to read in private and which were not performed on the stage. Seneca was one of the many Romans who had a very low opinion of actors and the theatre. One reason for this low esteem was that plays were put on in the Roman theatres as interludes between gladiatorial contests or fights between wild beasts and humans. Can you imagine plays being put on during half-time at a football game, or half-way through a boxing match?

This mixing of drama with the more popular and bloodier contests in the theatre disgusted the few Romans who hoped that they could treat the theatre and drama as seriously as the Greeks had done. In order to gain the attention of the crowds at the theatre, plays had to be of a very low standard – with plenty of buffoonery, low comedy or bloodletting. Actors were soon considered to be people of low intellect – who else would allow themselves to compete with lions and elephants for the applause of the crowds?

6 The Roman amphitheatre at Nîmes in France – a reminder of the days when the Roman Empire was at its height.

7 A circus entertains crowds in a Roman amphitheatre. During the interval plays were put on by actors to keep the audience amused. Notice how much grander this Roman amphitheatre is than the Greek theatres – a tribute to Roman skills in design and building.

8 (*Left*) An example of a Grecian mask worn by actors in the Roman theatre. This particular mask was found while the Roman theatre at Caerleon in Wales was being excavated.

9 (*Below*) A 'jongleresse' entertaining a noble lady with mime and song. Middle Ages.

We can get some impression of this from an account by the Roman writer, Tacitus, when commenting upon the Emperor Nero's ambition to become both a playwright and an actor:

> Seneca and Burrhus endeavoured to prevent the ridicule, to which a prince might expose himself by exhibiting his talents to the multitude. By their directions, a wide space, in the vale at the foot of the Vatican, was enclosed for the use of the emperor, that he might there manage the reins, and practise all his skill, without being a spectacle for the public eye. But his love of fame was not to be confined within those narrow bounds and he invited the multitude [to attend].
>
> The general corruption encouraged Nero to throw off all restraint. He mounted the stage, and became a public performer for the amusement of the people. With his harp in his hand, he entered the scene; he tuned the chords with a graceful air, and with delicate flourishes gave a prelude to his art. (Tacitus, *Annals*)

The Early Christian Church

During the fourth century AD the Christian Church became the official Church of the Roman state, with a Christian emperor encouraging his people to follow the new religion and give up their old gods. Because of actors' bad reputation, the Church forbade its members to go to the theatre; actors could not take part in any of the Church's ceremonies and were not allowed to receive any of the Church's blessings – such as a Christian wedding, a funeral or the baptism of their children.

In time, as the influence of the Church grew stronger, the theatre as the Greeks and earlier Romans had known it died out. The huge theatres fell into ruin or were used as market places; there were no schools where people could train to become actors or actresses; no-one wrote new plays, and nearly everybody accepted the teaching of the Church which so vigorously opposed the theatre.

Tradition Maintained

As we saw in Chapter 1, however, acting is a natural instinct for even the youngest children. Although there was no official theatre and no new plays were written for many centuries, men continued to travel around the countryside performing in one way or another. Troupes of acrobats, jugglers and tumblers amused the crowds at fairs and markets, and ballad singers or jongleurs went from town to town and castle to castle entertaining people with their songs, most of which were traditional stories about great heroes. These men, in a sense, were playwrights, and their ballads were, in a way, plays, although they were not usually written down.

The Church Changes its Mind

It is difficult to understand the opposition of the early Christian Church to the theatre, because so much of the Christian story can be adapted for dramatic purposes; after all, almost every junior school today produces its Christmas play. Equally, so much of the ritual of the Church – its processions and the costumes of its ministers at great ceremonies – is theatrical, since one of the purposes of the ritual and costumes is to arouse the emotion of the audience.

From about AD 900, however, the Church changed its attitude towards the theatre, and what it had once condemned it now took over. At first the actors were priests, who performed simple miracle plays. They used their churches as theatres, particularly at Easter and Christmas when they included in the special services a few brief scenes to illustrate the birth and death of Jesus. The plays were very simple. Later miracle plays told well-known Bible stories or tales of the saints and martyrs. Some priests introduced scenery into their 'plays', and one example of this can still be seen today. It was St Francis of Assisi (1182-1226) who built the first Christmas crib, around which actors represented Mary, Joseph, the three kings and the shepherds who came to worship the infant Jesus.

In some plays, however, the actors had to move from place to place, and many plays had a very large cast. Soon the churches were no longer suitable theatres for these new plays and by about AD 1100 most miracle plays were being performed in the square in front of the church, or in some cases in special buildings. We know that this was so in London. William Fitzstephen, writing during the reign of Henry II (1154-89) noted:

> But London, for the shows upon theatres and comical pastimes, hath holy plays, representations of miracles which holy confessors have wrought, or representations of torments wherein the constancy of martyrs appeared.

Notice the words 'shows upon theatres', which indicate that, in London at least, there were several such buildings. Notice also the type of plays performed.

It is a little ironic that the Church, which had in its earliest days condemned the theatre, was now, in the twelfth century, using drama to arouse the emotions for what was considered a holy purpose. Even more ironical was the fact that many of these plays were used in the monastery schools as teaching aids, to help the students understand their Bible history and Church history all the better.

10 (*Opposite*) An angel appears before the shepherds to tell them of Jesus's coming – a reconstruction of a medieval miracle play. Notice how the performance is taking place inside the church. Later, as plays grew more elaborate, they would move out into the market square.

Chapter 4. Morality Plays – the Layman's Theatre Again

Lay Actors

When the miracle plays moved out into the church squares and, in some cases, into theatres, the Church authorities decided that it was not right for priests to continue to be actors. What had seemed to be right inside the church was condemned when the drama moved outside. So priests were replaced by lay actors. At about the same time, the language of the plays began to change. The priests had given their sermons, and acted their miracle plays, in Latin; and at first the lay actors continued to use that language – which was spoken by educated people everywhere in Europe. But late in the twelfth century they began to give their plays in the language of the country – English laymen delivered their plays in English.

Each age, as we have seen, has its own theatre. Between 1300 and 1500, the theatre reflected the growing nationalism of different countries – hence the increasing use of the native language instead of Latin. The acting of laymen instead of priests was a reflection of the increasing confidence of ordinary people, who were no longer quite as willing to accept the rules of the Church – particularly in worldly matters, such as trade, business and entertainment.

The Guilds

One sign of this increasing confidence among ordinary people was the formation of trade guilds. To understand this development we must remember that thirteenth-century England was a mainly agricultural country, in which

11 (*Opposite*) The joyous celebration of Christmas in medieval England, when the Lord of the Manor abdicated in favour of a Lord of Misrule, or Christmas Prince, whose reign extended over the 12 days of Christmas. Such a tradition of buffoonery and merry-making was later incorporated into the lay theatre.

most people earned their living from farming. It was also a thinly populated country, with a population of a mere three million or so. These people lived in villages or small market towns. Apart from London there were no large towns. The bigger towns – such as York, Chester and Norwich – were protected by enormous stone walls, the remains of which can be seen at Chester and York in particular.

In these small towns there were a number of men who followed particular trades – 'butcher, baker and candlestick maker'. Each trade had its own guild, to which every tradesman belonged. So, in York, there was one guild for the goldsmiths and another for the York carpenters. Men joined these guilds for many reasons. Out of the contributions they made to the guild's funds they would receive help when they were sick, out of work or too old to work any longer; and when they died, members of the guild would offer masses for their soul and pray regularly for them, and would also provide money to help the dead man's wife and children. Although laymen were becoming more independent, they were still very religious, and this was important for the development of the theatre, as we shall see.

The Cycle of Plays

Each guild helped to celebrate the major feasts of the Church by putting on a play and, in time, there grew up a number of 'cycles of plays'. At York, for example, 49 different plays were put on by the different guilds on the same day in the small, walled town. In Wakefield there were 32 plays in the 'cycle', in Chester 25 and in Coventry 42. They were called 'cycles' because they took their audiences on a journey from 'the Creation of the World to the Coronation

12 Christ Harrowing Hell – a favourite subject of mystery plays. The porter of Hell (*on the right*) is blowing a blast on his trumpet to arouse the fiendish hosts. This illustration is based on an early manuscript of one of the Chester mystery plays.

of the Blessed Virgin in Heaven'. Each guild was asked to put on the appropriate play for a portion of this story – or cycle. Thus, in York, the glaziers' guild performed 'The Harrowing of Hell', while the more fortunate goldsmiths' guild acted the story of the Three Wise Men on their journey to and from Bethlehem.

The collection of plays was also known as a 'cycle' because each guild took its play around the streets of the town, repeating its performance at a number of fixed 'stations'. In York there were 12 such stations where the crowd could gather to watch first one play and then another, until they had seen each of the 49 plays in the York cycle – and all this without moving, and all in the course of one day.

The plays in the cycle were at first concerned with some Biblical text – the life of Christ or of one of the saints. They were more extravagant productions of the old miracle plays, and were meant to remind people of their religious duties. The theatres were usually wagons, of which each guild had its own. This is how a writer in the fifteenth century described the wagons in the Chester cycle:

> The maner of these playes [the Whitsun plays at Chester] weare every company [craft guilds] had his pagiant, a high scafolde with 2 rowmes, a higher and a lower, upon 4 wheels. In the lower they apparelled themselves,

> and in the higher rowme they played, beinge all open on the tope, that all behoulders might heare and see them. The places where they played them was in every streete. They begane first at the Abay gates, and when the first pagiant was played it was wheeled to the high crosse before the Mayor, and so to every streete, and soe every streete had a pagiant playeinge before them at one time, till all the pagiantes for the daye appoynted weare played, and when one pagiant was neere ended worde was broughte from streete to streete, that soe they might come in place thereof, exceedinge orderlye, and all the streetes have their pagiantes afore them all at one time and playeinge togeather; to se w'ch playes was great resorte, and also scafoldes and stages made in the streetes in those places where they determined to playe theire pagiantes.

Notice the reference in the last sentence to 'scafoldes and stages' being set up at points 'where they were determined to play theire pagiantes'. It is not clear from this whether, in fact, there were stages as we understand them – on which the actors played out their play – or whether the 'scafoldes and stages' refer to some sort of seating arrangement, which would have been needed if a large number of people were to see the various plays.

A cycle of plays being performed at about twelve different points in the town meant that a person who wanted to see the whole cycle would have to stay in one place from sunrise to sunset. The guilds realized that they could not expect to hold the attention of the crowd for a whole day if every play was deadly serious, and the most popular plays were those which provided a touch of comedy. One of these was *Noah's Flood*, part of the Chester cycle. Noah's wife refused to go into the Ark unless she could take her gossipy women friends with her. The row between her and the patient Noah, the way in which her sons carried her into the Ark, and the fight which she put up against them all pleased the crowds – particularly since the part of Noah's wife was played by a man, rather like the part of the Dame in a modern pantomime.

The Pageant and its Players

Each guild had its own pageant master – or director. It was his job to choose men to play the various parts, to hire the craftsmen from the town to make the scenery and costumes and to arrange rehearsals. We must remember that the people who took part in these plays were amateur and not professional actors. Throughout the year they earned their living from their trade – as bakers, arrow-makers or silversmiths. They only became actors for a short period before the pageant. Thus they resembled the members of the many thousands of amateur groups in modern Britain, who put on performances of plays old and new in church, town and village halls, and find in these amateur theatricals a great relief from their day-to-day tasks.

13 (*Above left*) A mystery play showing the martyrdom of a saint. Fourteenth century.

14 (*Above right*) A mystery play being performed in Chester.

15 (*Opposite*) Behind the scenes of hell – an artist's impression of the performance of a fifteenth-century mystery play, showing the people who worked backstage to produce the sound effects, the flames and the smoke.

However, the guild did pay its players for their part in the miracle play. Records show that the person who played the part of God in the Coventry cycle received 17½p as his wage. He was luckier than the man who played God in the Hull cycle. He only received 4p – a sign that Coventry was a richer place than Hull in medieval times. You may think that this was not much of a wage for a hard-worked actor to receive. But remember that, in those days, a skilled craftsman was paid about 2p a day, while an unskilled workman received only ½p. Bearing these wages in mind, you can see that the Coventry God was well paid for his work.

The pageant master was given a copy of the guild's play by the master of the guild, to whom it was returned for safekeeping once the pageant was ended. Today we would expect every actor to be given a copy of the play in which he

16 The modern Lord Mayor's Show, a weak reflection of the pageants of earlier times.

was appearing – or at least a typewritten copy of his part. But in medieval times there were no typewriters and no printing. The pageant master had to copy out the script by hand. It should also be remembered that few, if any, of the actors were able to read.

Rehearsals, therefore, consisted largely of the pageant master reciting the lines, while the actors, listening intently, tried to memorize them. For two or three weeks before the cycle was due to be played, there were long sessions of such rehearsals with the pageant master driving his actors to become word perfect.

Meanwhile, the wagon on which the play was to be acted was taken from the pageant house where it had been kept sheltered from the weather. It was freshly painted, its wheels were greased so that it ran smoothly, and the stage was erected so that it would stand firm while the wagon rolled over the cobbled streets.

Elsewhere in the town the costumes were being made. These were a very costly item in the budget of the pageant master – and of the guild which paid him. Sometimes a guild would get some of this money back by hiring out its costumes to people in neighbouring parishes, who wanted to put on a play but did not have the money to make their own costumes.

As well as costumes for the actors, curtains and other decorations had to be prepared for the pageant. Even the horses that dragged the pageant through the streets were bedecked in decorative outfits. Sometimes a guild's pageant might only need one or two horses for this purpose, but the pageants of the wealthier guilds, who put on large and impressive displays, were long and heavy contraptions which might require as many as six horses. Each of these had to be carefully groomed and decorated before the great day.

So everywhere in the town there was active preparation for the cycle – actors were rehearsing, costume-makers were sewing and stitching, and carpenters were busy with scenery and scaffolds. In case anyone remained unaware of what was going on, the town council paid for heralds to go through the narrow streets blowing their trumpets and announcing the various attractions that would be displayed at the forthcoming cycle. All this helped to build up great excitement in the town and made the cycle a memorable part of the year.

The Cornish Cycle

A great deal has been written about the York, Chester, Coventry and Wakefield cycles. Much less has been written about the Cornish cycle – which is important for several reasons. Firstly, the Cornish cycle was performed in ancient theatres possibly built by the Druids. One Cornish writer, Borlase, noted:

> Where these stone enclosures are semi-circular, and distinguished by seats and benches of like materials, there is no doubt they were constructed in that form for the convenience of the spectators at plays, games, and festivals. There is a theatre of this kind in Anglesea, resembling a horseshoe, including an area of twenty-two paces diameter, called Bryngwyn [or Supreme Court], with its opening to the west. It lies in a place called Tre'r Drew [or Druid's Town], from whence it may be reasonably conjectured that this kind of structure was used by the Druids . . .
>
> We have one whose benches are of stone, and the most remarkable monument of this kind which I have yet seen; it is near the Church of St Just, Penwith. It was an exact circle, of 126 feet diameter; the perpendicular height of the bank, from the area within, now 7 feet high; but the height from the bottom of the ditch without, 10 feet at present, formerly more. The seats consist of six steps 14 inches wide and 1 foot high, with one on the top of all, where the rampart is about 7 feet wide.
>
> The plays they acted in these amphitheatres were in the Cornish language; the subjects taken from Scripture history.

No doubt there were similar plays, in similar open-air theatres, performed in

¶Here begynneth a treatyse how ẏ hye
fader of heuen sendeth dethe to so-
mon euery creature to come and
gyue a counte of theyr lyues in
this worlde/and is in maner
of a morall playe.

other parts of Christian England – particularly on the new Feast of Corpus Christi, on the Thursday after Trinity Sunday. This holy-day was introduced in 1264 by Pope Urban IV, who was anxious that the faithful should remember the way in which Christ had celebrated the Last Supper. The day on which the Supper took place – Holy Thursday – was the day before Good Friday and the solemn preparations for the sad ceremonies of the Friday meant that people were unable to celebrate the Feast of the Supper in a fitting way. After 1264, in the English midsummer, there was a new feast day – yet another holiday from work – and a chance to celebrate with games and festivities of all sorts, including the cycle of plays.

Other Theatres

We know that by the end of the fourteenth century there were a number of theatres, often near a church, where plays were performed. One was described by a medieval historian as:

> curbed about with hard stone, not far from the west end of Clerkenwell Church. The church took the name of the well, and the well took the name of the parish clerks in London, who were accustomed there yearly to assemble, and to play some large history of Holy Scripture. And for example of later time – to wit, in the year 1390, the 14th of Richard II – I read the parish Clerks of London, on the 18th of July, played interludes, at Skinners' Well, near unto Clerkes' Well, which play continued three days together, the king, queen and nobles being present. Also in the year 1409, the 10th of Henry IV, they played a play at the Skinners' Well, which lasted eight days, and was of matter from the creation of the world.

The Morality Plays

The pageants of the York, Chester and other cycles were part of the Christian life of a Christian country. It is hard for us to appreciate how these cycles appeared to the people; we have a very weak reflection of the cycle in the modern Lord Mayor's Show in London. Here there are a number of different groups, each putting on some sort of show on its separate wagon. But no-one stops, there is no acting, and the theme of the pageant is usually some very materialist item like 'London serves the world of trade' or 'Britain can make it' – a far cry from the cycle of miracle plays.

Even in medieval times men became dissatisfied with miracle plays and demanded something different. They were then presented with morality plays – in which the emphasis was no longer on Christ, the saints or scripture but on the lives of ordinary people. However, this is not to say that morality plays

17 (*Opposite*) The title page of *Everyman*, one of the finest English morality plays. Sixteenth century.

were like a modern TV drama. The plays were written and watched by people who were very conscious of the truths of their religion. The morality plays consisted of stories of the struggle between good and evil in ordinary people's lives. One description of a morality play says that it is the story of:

> Human Nature tempted by Luxury, saved by Potentia, taken to the Castle of Perseverance where it is again tempted by Avarice but saved again by Pity and Mercy.

Each of the virtues and vices which struggle for the soul of man was personified by an actor, and the dramatist endeavoured to teach the audience that they should reject evil and cooperate with God and virtue; otherwise, when they come to die they will say:

> *Alas, whereto may I trust?*
> *Beauty goeth fast away from me;*
> *She promised with me to live and die.*

These lines are from *Everyman,* the finest of the morality plays, and one which is still performed today.

The Decline of the Morality Play

Each age has its own theatre and the morality play suited people of a certain age. After the Reformation of the sixteenth century, however, there was less need for such plays. They had been dramatic forms of sermons. Now, in Protestant churches, the preachers gave very long sermons each Sunday — enough to last most men for a week. They therefore wanted something different in their theatre, something more entertaining. This gave rise to the interlude — a short play presented in between some other form of entertainment.

The interludes were performed by strolling bands of actors who, accompanied by musicians, tumblers and acrobats, took their shows from castle to castle and town to town. Unknowingly, these groups made an important contribution to the next major step in the history of the theatre. Where would these players stay when they arrived at a town but in one of the many local inns? And where better to get a ready-made audience for their performance than in the courtyard of that inn? These were quite large open spaces, where rich people left their horses to be stabled and where luggage was kept, surrounded on at least three sides by various inn buildings. These buildings provided a ready-made arrangement for seating the audience, and the courtyard below provided an excellent stage.

Chapter 5. The Renaissance and the Theatre

The Renaissance

In the last chapter we saw that in the thirteenth century, with plays such as *Everyman*, dramatists were beginning to write more about man himself and less about Bible stories. This interest in man was part of the movement to which we

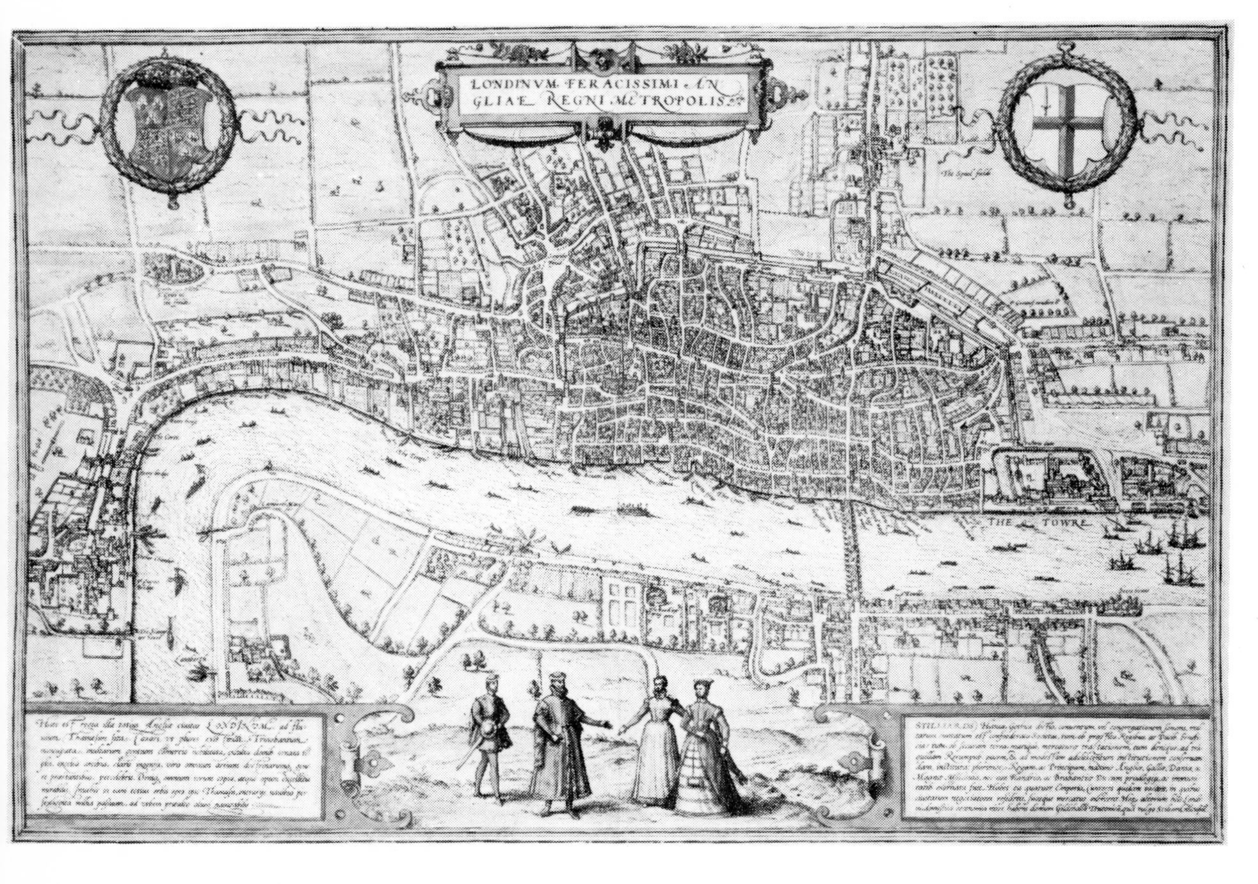

18 A bird's eye view of sixteenth-century London, showing Whitehall and Westminster on the left and the Tower on the right. This small city was encompassed by walls running north and north-west from the Tower.

give the name Renaissance, which began in the thirteenth century and was both the result and the cause of major religious, political, scientific and intellectual changes.

You have probably read about the great discoveries that were made by the intrepid explorers of this period (1400-1600), such as Ferdinand Magellan, Vasco da Gama, Christopher Columbus and John Cabot. Between them, they discovered many new lands and opened up the world to trade on a scale that men had never previously dreamed of. The work of these sailors was part of the Renaissance. Man learned that he could do great things, could invent new equipment to help him sail around the world, could open up new lands and horizons. The explorers also showed that a good deal of what had previously been taught – about the shape of the world for example – was nonsense, and in so doing encouraged others to challenge long-standing ideas. More and more people began to question what had previously been uncritically accepted – in the name of freedom of thought.

This freedom and the achievements of the discoverers added to the dignity of man in general. Whereas before men had been taught to think of themselves mainly as future inhabitants of the Kingdom of Heaven, they now became more conscious of their life on earth and more aware of their dignity as human beings. This is reflected in the work of the great artists. In the past artists had produced pictures of biblical scenes only – and even in these the human bodies of the saints or of the Blessed Virgin were relatively poorly painted. Now artists tried to show that the bodies of the saints were in themselves very precious and wonderful things. Michelangelo, Raphael, Leonardo da Vinci and other great Renaissance painters took immense pride in painting saints, Christs and Blessed Virgins who looked like very real, human beings – and not some wishy-washy product of a mind that was more concerned with heaven than with man on earth. Even more significant is the fact that many of these artists began to paint pictures of ordinary people; Leonardo's famous 'Mona Lisa' and Holbein's 'Henry VIII' are two examples of the many thousands of portraits which were painted of kings, dukes, courtiers, merchants and scholars.

A New Theatre

Who paid for these paintings of ordinary people? In the past there had been a few wealthy, noble landowners and a smaller number of merchants and traders, but with the discovery and opening up of new lands many merchants and traders, shipyard owners and bankers benefited from increased trade and grew very rich.

We can describe these people as a new, rich middle class. Unlike the upper-class landowner, they made their money from trade and industry; unlike the lower class of worker, they had so much money that they could afford to live like the landowner, spending vast sums on houses, paintings, decorations

19 The Old Bull & Mouth Inn, St Martins-le-Grand, London. From this Victorian engraving you can get some idea of the size of the yards in which plays were performed in the sixteenth century, with the audience packed along the balconies of the inn.

and furniture. They were proud to be the patrons of the new artists – and of the new dramatists.

Painting and sculpture flourished as a result of the Renaissance. So, too, did the theatre. Spain was then the world's richest country and in Madrid, Seville, Valencia and other towns and cities the new middle class paid for the building of huge theatres, in which a new breed of producer employed painters to provide him with movable, painted scenery. There was also a new breed of dramatist, who wrote plays that the new patrons would welcome, such as comedies and uncomplicated stories based on history or the achievements of famous people. The best known of these new playwrights was Lope de Vega (1562-1635) who wrote more than 500 plays, many of them in verse.

20 Sir Francis Walsingham, one of Elizabeth's chief ministers and the licensee of a group of actors (*see* pages 39-40).

England and the Renaissance Theatre

In the fifteenth century, England was not one of the leading powers of Europe. The country was being ravaged by the Wars of the Roses, as the upper-class followers of the House of York battled relentlessly against the upper-class followers of the House of Lancaster. Spain, France, Venice, Genoa and Florence were all richer and more powerful than England, and it was in these countries and city-states that came the first new moves in exploration and painting. But some of this climate of change filtered through to England where, by 1500, the Lancastrian Henry Tudor sat securely on the throne. The discovery of gunpowder, and the invention of the cannon, now made the nobleman's castle obsolete as a defence in wartime, and the upper classes gave up their warring and turned their castles into more comfortable homes. There, like the European middle class, they employed painters, architects and furniture makers to improve their living conditions.

At the same time, England began to share in the increased trade between Europe and the Americas and a new, rich middle class of merchants and traders, financiers and lawyers grew up. These men lived in the towns and not in country castles, and it was they who provided the main support for the development of an English theatre.

English Theatre in the Sixteenth Century

As late as 1575 there was no building specially designed as a theatre; actors performed in private houses, at the King's Court, or in the yards of inns. The Protestants who now controlled London's city council were opposed to anyone building a theatre for reasons which we shall see. One contemporary writer noted:

> 1572. Plaies are banished for a time out of London, lest the resort unto them should ingender a plague, or rather disperse it, being already begonne. Would to God these common plaies were exiled for altogether, as siminaries of impiety, and no better than houses of bawdrie. It is an evident token of a wicked time, when plaiers waxe so riche.

The players referred to in this extract had, by law, to belong to a company of actors. But no-one could just decide to form a theatrical company. People who wanted to put on a play had to follow one of three paths. They could apply to the local magistrates for permission to form a company to perform plays in the locality over which the magistrates had power. They could also apply to a nobleman, who had the right to nominate one company of his own. Thus there was the Earl of Warwick's Company, for instance, and the Earl of Southampton's Company. These companies performed for the noblemen and their friends, but were also free to travel the country putting on their plays in

21 James Burbage's son, Richard, chief actor and manager of the Lord Chamberlain's Company. He was three years younger than William Shakespeare, and Shakespeare wrote many of his tragic parts with Burbage in mind.

places where the magistrates allowed them.

A company could also try to gain a licence from the monarch, and so become a Company of the King's (or Queen's) Players. They would provide entertainment for the sovereign and the Court, but were also free to put on plays in other towns and cities if they could get permission from the local magistrates. Actors and playwrights were fortunate that Elizabeth I (1558-1603) enjoyed the theatre; and when the various companies faced opposition in London they invited the Queen and her council to help them. One letter from the Queen's Council to the London council reads:

> My lords think it would not be unfit at that time to allow the players in the city, in respect that her majesty sometimes took delight in those pastimes, and that they might thereby attain more dexterity and perfection in that profession, the better to content her majesty. It is suggested that they be restrained from playing on the Sabbath, and only permitted on the ordinary holidays after evening prayer. If the exercise of the plays should increase the sickness and infection, the lord mayor should communicate to the council. My lords also suggest that the city should appoint some proper person to consider and allow such plays only as were fitted to yield honest recreation and no example of evil.

The First English Theatre

If these companies of actors received permission to put on a performance, they then had to find somewhere to perform. The usual place was in the yard of one or other of the many large inns, which offered an open space where the play could be performed and ready-made seating for the audience on the overhanging balconies.

In 1574, James Burbage had formed a company of players and received a licence from the Earl of Leicester. Burbage and his company put on various plays in different inn-yards, but by 1576 Burbage had discovered two problems. Firstly, the company had to rely on the generosity of the audience for their income; there was no way in which they could charge admission money to the people already in the inn, who were able to watch the play from a balcony. Secondly, the innkeepers charged a fee for the companies to use their yards. So Burbage and his men were not getting a fair return for the work they put in.

Burbage began to look around for a place where, like the Spaniards, he could build a permanent theatre. He knew that there was no chance of the London council giving him permission to build one in the city itself. He also knew that just outside the city walls, in Shoreditch, there were large open spaces where for many years Londoners had gone to enjoy archery, handball, football, wrestling, cockfighting and, as one royal proclamation put it, 'such like vain

22 The three-storey Curtain Theatre, from an engraving made about 1600. By this time Burbage's Theatre had been moved to the South Bank and the Curtain stood alone as a place of entertainment in Shoreditch Fields. Notice the flag flying – a signal to Londoners that there would be a performance that day.

plays which have no profit in them'. There was also in that area a former monastery, now closed as a result of the Reformation, which had been built near a holy well. The district was later called Halliwell.

We have already seen that there was a close connection between the Church and early forms of drama. We have also seen that in Roman times, as well as in the Middle Ages, there was a tradition that the play was only one of many forms of entertainment which people enjoyed – at the same place and on the same day. So it was fairly natural for Burbage to build the first English theatre at Shoreditch, on a site which was only about one mile from the City of London and to which Londoners could go via Cripplegate, Moorgate or Bishopsgate.

Burbage paid £666 for the construction of his theatre. Here the company

23 An artist's impression of a performance at the Fortune Theatre, 1611. The Puritan London council was afraid that the bawdy behaviour of the actors would incite a riot in the city.

put on their plays, charging an admission fee of one penny, and within a short time they had made a great deal of money. This showed that the Puritan-minded London council were not speaking for the city's people when they condemned theatres, plays and actors. Londoners flocked to Burbage's theatre and his success soon encouraged others to build. Within a short time there was a rival on the site – the Curtain Theatre – although Burbage's building retained the proud title of 'The Theatre'.

We know a good deal about the details of The Theatre. We know, for example, that it was round – rather like the Globe Theatre described by Shakespeare in the Prologue to *Henry V*:

> *. . . but pardon gentles all,*
> *The flat unraised spirits that have dared*
> *On this unworthy scaffold to bring forth*

So great an object: can this cockpit hold
The vasty fields of France? or may we cram
Within the wooden O the very casques
That did affright the air at Agincourt?

Notice the reference to the theatre being a 'wooden O' and the comparison between the theatre and a 'cockpit'. Not all sixteenth-century theatres were this shape – others were rectangular. But the Burbage Theatre, the Curtain and many other later theatres were circular or semi-circular in shape. Notice also in illustration 27 the similarity between the theatre and the yards of inns where the players had once performed.

The Council and the Theatre

Although the London council had no power to act against Burbage and his Theatre, since it was outside the city walls, they continued to oppose him. In due course they persuaded the magistrates of Middlesex to act for them, and one indictment against Burbage and his company reads as follows:

> Middlesex, to wit: The Jurors for the Lady the Queen present that John Braynes of Shorditche in the county of Middlesex, yeoman, and James Burbage of the same [parish], yeoman, on the 21st day of February 1577 . . . brought together unlawful assemblies of the people to hear and see certain plays practised by the same John Braynes and James Burbage and others at a place called The Theatre in Hallywell in the aforesaid county. By reason of which unlawful assembly of the people great affrays, assaults, tumults and quasi-insurrections . . . have been done by very many ill-disposed persons, to the great disturbance of the peace of the Lady the Queen and the overthrowing of good order and rule.

Notice the assumption in the indictment that the theatre produced unruly behaviour in the crowds. The London council also blamed theatres for the spread of various diseases and, in June 1580, it wrote to the Queen asking for her help:

> for the redress of such things as were found dangerous in spreading the infection and otherwise drawing God's wrath and plague upon the city, such as the erecting and frequenting of infamous houses out of the liberties and jurisdiction of the city, the drawing of the people from the service of God and honest exercises, to unchaste plays.

In 1583 the Lord Mayor wrote to Sir Francis Walsingham, one of the Queen's chief advisers, informing him that the London council had decided to

24 London Bridge which linked the South Bank (*in the foreground*) with the City of London.

take certain action to help stamp out the plague:

> Among other great inconveniences were the assemblies of people to plays, bear-baiting, fencers, and profane spectacles at The Theatre and Curtain and other like places, to which great multitudes of the worst sort of people resorted.

Walsingham, who had his own licensed company, proved to be a friend to The Theatre and to actors in general. As the historian, Stow, wrote in 1615:

> Comedians and stage-players of former time were very poore and ignorant in respect of these of this time, but being now growne very skilfull and exquisite Actors for all matters, they were entertained into the service of divers great lords, out of which Companies there were xii of the best chosen, and at the request of Sir Francis Walsingham they were sworn the Queenes servants, and were allowed wages and liveries as groomes of the chamber . . .

The London council would hesitate before acting against 'the Queenes servants'.

Shakespeare Arrives

William Shakespeare arrived in London in 1585 and worked in Burbage's Theatre – first for Burbage himself and then, by 1594, as a member of the Lord Chamberlain's Company. In December 1594 the Company performed before the Queen at Greenwich Palace, as this extract from the accounts of the Queen's Private Treasurer shows:

> To William Kempe, William Shakespeare, and Richard Burbage, servants to the Lord Chamberleyne, for twoe severall comedies or interludes shewed by them before her Majestie in Christmas tyme laste paste, viz: ypon St Stephen's daye and Innocentes daye, xiijli, vjs, viijd [£12 5s 7d = £12.28], and by waye of her Majestie's rewarde, vjli, xiijs, iiijd [£5 12s 3d = £5.61].

But pressure from the London council continued and on 28 July 1597 the Queen's Council issued an order to the Middlesex magistrates to close The Theatre and other playhouses in their district.

As a result Burbage was forced to move his Theatre to the other bank of the Thames – to the South Bank or Surrey side – where there were already a number of other playhouses and centres of entertainment. It is with the South Bank that Shakespeare's name is intimately connected – a new, great era in English theatre was about to begin.

Chapter 6. Shakespeare

The Spirit of the Age

In 1588 the Spanish Armada was sent on its ill-fated attempt to invade England, to overthrow Elizabeth I and instal a Spanish King on the throne. The defeat of the Armada sparked off a great wave of patriotism which symbolized the coming-of-age of England, as a nation, and as a force in European politics.

It cannot be dismissed as accidental that at this time, circa 1590-1620, there was more dramatic talent in England than there has ever been before or since. It was the age of Christopher Marlowe, Shakespeare's predecessor and a writer

25 William Shakespeare, by Droeshout.

of tragedies; of Ben Jonson, the author of great comedies; of Thomas Dekker, the creator of romantic roles for women; of Thomas Middleton and Thomas Heywood, John Webster and Philip Massinger, Francis Beaumont and Phineas Fletcher. And, above all, it was the age of the towering genius of William Shakespeare. It is little wonder that Dr Rowse, the historian of Elizabeth I and her times, compares London in this period to Athens at its peak. Successful in war, trade and industry, London – like ancient Athens – produced great theatre.

The Plays and Their Audience

For the theatrical companies, to gain the friendship of the Queen and some of her courtiers was a safeguard against attack by local councils – dominated, as so many councils were, by the extreme Protestants known as Puritans. To help maintain that friendship between courtier and company, playwrights went out of their way to write into their plays lines that would please the Queen and her Court. There was a constant appeal to people to obey the law and honour their country.

26 (*Below left*) The Globe Theatre, from Visscher's *View of London* published in 1616.

27 (*Below right*) The interior of the Swan Theatre, drawn by John de Witt in 1596. It is the only authentic drawing that remains of an Elizabethen theatre. Notice the similarities with the inn-yard (picture **19** page 31), the flag showing that a performance was about to take place, the apron stage and the lack of scenery.

This is very well illustrated in Shakespeare's play *Henry V.* Shakespeare's friend and patron was the Earl of Southampton, who was General of the Horse in the army which the Queen's favourite – the Earl of Essex – was to lead against the rebels in Ireland. The expedition left for Ireland in March 1599. Just after this departure Shakespeare wrote the stirring and patriotic *Henry V.* In this play there are references to the popularity of Essex among the people of London and also to the eagerness with which they waited for news of his victory over the rebellious Irish. This must have made pleasing material for an evening's entertainment in one of the royal palaces, and would have drawn the approving nods of the Queen, Southampton, Essex and other noblemen towards the playwright and his company.

The playwright had to be aware not only of the Court but had also to consider the tastes of the people who, he hoped, were going to pay to come and see the play – and so make him rich. On one level – in the expensive seats in the covered gallery – an educated group of playgoers waited to be entertained. They probably approved of the patriotism behind plays such as *Henry V,* and appreciated the subtle humour of a play containing lines such as:

Sweet mistress, whereas I love you nothing at all,
Regarding your substance and riches chief of all;
For your personage, beauty, demeanour and wit,
I commend me unto you never a whit.

This extract is from a play by Nicolas Udall, a former headmaster of Eton. The wrong punctuation in the lines – which the more educated were able to appreciate – was borrowed by Shakespeare for *A Midsummer Night's Dream.*

But there were also the less educated crowds who paid their single penny to stand in the open, unless they were lucky enough to grab one of the few stools. For these, Shakespeare and other playwrights had to provide broad comedy, and plenty of rough entertainment such as wrestling, sword-fighting and bloodletting. Sometimes, as with the Porter's scene in *Macbeth,* a comic character is introduced into the middle of a very serious play – as if the writer were conscious that the majority of people would be unwilling to watch a play that was deadly serious all the time. Again, in *As You Like It,* the playwright asks his characters to indulge in wrestling, as if he knew that most of his audience would soon grow tired of the romantic theme of the play.

The Globe Theatre

In December 1598, Burbage's lease expired and he was forced to close The Theatre in Shoreditch. One of the terms of the lease was that Burbage, who had paid for the building of The Theatre, had the right to pull it down when the lease expired. In December 1598 he did just that, much to the anger of the landowner, Allen, who took out a summons against Burbage for:

> unlawfully combyninge and confederating himself with the sayd Richard Burbage and one Peter Streat, William Smyth, and divers other persons, to the number of twelve, to your subject unknowne, did aboute the eight and twentyth daye of December, ryoutouslye assemble themselves together, and then and there armed themselves with divers and manye unlawfull and offensive weapons, as namelye, swordes, daggers, billes, axes, and such like, and soe armed, did then repayre unto the sayd Theater, and then and there, armed as aforesayd, in verye ryotous, outragious and forcyble manner, and contrarye to the lawes of your highnes realme, attempted to pull downe the sayd Theater to the greate disturbance and terrefying of your Majesties loving subjects there neere inhabitinge; and having so done, did then alsoe in most forcyble and ryotous manner take and carrye away from thence all the wood and timber thereof unto the Bancksyde in the parishe of St Mary Overyes, and there erected a newe playhouse with the sayd timber and wood.

The 'newe playhouse' on 'the Bancksyde' was the Globe Theatre, with which most of Shakespeare's great plays are associated. We have several illustrations of the exterior of this theatre, which show nearby a bearpit and other centres of rough entertainment. But we have no contemporary illustrations of the interior of the Globe. We do, however, have a drawing of the inside of the Swan Theatre which dates from 1596 – the only surviving illustration of the interior of an Elizabethan theatre. We also have a description of the interior, written in 1599 by T Platter in his *Travels in England.* Platter wrote:

> Daily at two in the afternoon, London has two, sometimes three plays running . . . and those which play best obtain most spectators. The playhouses are so constructed that they play on a raised platform, so that everyone has a good view. There are different galleries where the seating is more comfortable and therefore more expensive. For whoever cares to stand below only pays one English penny, but if he wishes to sit, he enters by another door, and pays another penny, while if he desires to sit in the most comfortable seats, which are cushioned, where he not only sees everything well, but can also be seen, he pays yet another . . . And during the performance food and drink are carried round the audience. The actors are most expensively and elaborately costumed; for it is the English usage for

28 (*Opposite*) An artist's impression of a performance at the Fortune Theatre. Notice the man on the left who, like many Elizabethan theatre-goers, is staving off his hunger with an apple.

29 A play in progress at the Red Bull Playhouse. Notice how the audience are all around the stage.

eminent Lords or Knights to bequeath and leave almost the best of their clothes to their serving men, which it is unseemly for the latter to wear, so they offer them then for sale for a small sum to the actors.

Notice the different seats mentioned for the different classes in the audience. Those who paid only a penny and stayed on the ground floor were referred to as 'groundlings', while the better-off in their galleried seats were known as 'the gods'. Notice also the 'food and drink' – an almost modern reference you might think. But the Elizabethan theatre-goers used to eat cooked meats, bowls of stew or soup and other hot, messy dishes during the performance. They also bought great quantities of nuts, and there is constant reference in letters and diaries to the smells in the theatre, and to the noise made by those who cracked and ate the nuts and those who then crushed the shells as they walked around the place – all very different from the almost reverential hush in a modern theatre.

The Stage

The stage in Elizabethan theatres was apron-shaped, sticking out into the auditorium where the groundlings stood on all three sides of it. The actors and the play were very much part of the audience who, in turn, were very involved in the action that was taking place. There was no curtain, and on the whole no scenery. At the back of the stage a covered portion allowed the actors to play scenes that were supposed to be taking place indoors, and over this there was a balcony used, for example, in the famous love scene in *Romeo and Juliet.* However, the main purpose of the building at the back of the stage was to hold the costumes and other equipment that the actors needed for their various parts.

Many of us have grown up with TV as part of our lives, and so are used to seeing plays in which the camera presents us with wonderful scenery. But in Shakespeare's time the device of the painted scene – already in use in Spain (*see* Chapter 5) – had not yet been adopted in England. Instead the playwright had to ask his audience to use their imagination – as we have to do today if we listen to a radio play. Thus, in *Henry V,* the second act is introduced with the words:

. . . and the scene
Is now transported, gentles, to Southampton;
There is the playhouse now, there must you sit:
And thence to France shall we convey you safe,
And bring you back, charming the narrow seas
To give you gentle pass; for, if we may,
We'll not offend one stomach with our play,
But, till the king come forth, and not till then,
Unto Southampton do we shift our scene.

Later we are asked to pretend that on the small stage, with a handful of actors, we are going to witness the great Battle of Agincourt. As the play says:

And so our scene must to the battle fly;
Where – O for pity – we shall much disgrace . . .
The name of Agincourt. Yet sit and see,
Minding true things by what their mockeries be.

The Actors

Elizabethan actors were often part-owners of the theatres in which they played or of the companies to which they belonged. Instead of receiving a wage they took a share of the profits the company made from a performance. An important member of the company – one of the leading actors for example – might receive as much as a quarter share of the profits, while a new or junior member might only have a twentieth share. This profit-sharing system inspired the members of the company to work as hard as possible, in order to attract a large audience to their plays.

Alas it is my son Horatio.
Murder helpe Hieronimo
stop her mouth

There were about ten theatres in Elizabethan London, each trying to attract an audience; and, as we have seen, London then was not the thickly populated, widely spread city that it has become today. It was confined within the old city walls and its population was relatively small. So how could a company regularly attract a large audience to its theatre? One way was to put on plays which people would want to see – such as patriotic and anti-Spanish plays, great historical dramas or light comedies, each of which appealed to a different type of audience. Another way of ensuring regular audiences was to change plays fairly frequently. For two or three afternoons a company might perform, for example, Marlowe's *Tamburlaine*, and then for the other three afternoons in the week it would put on a comedy. The following week two more different plays would be acted, and then two more until the company felt that it was safe to put on *Tamburlaine* once again.

The men who acted in these many plays and performed day after day had received no training for their work. There was no Royal Academy of Dramatic Art (RADA) to which aspiring young actors could go to learn their trade. If a young man, like William Shakespeare in his youth, wanted to become an actor, he had to try and join a company. If accepted, he was at first employed at some menial task. It is said that Shakespeare's first job was to look after the horses of the richer patrons who came to the theatre. Later, if the boy was lucky, he might be given a small part in a play – when an actor was ill perhaps, or when a new play was being put on which had a larger cast than usual. If he had any natural ability as an actor, and if the leading members of the company allowed him, such a young man might then work his way up to playing more important parts.

One day, with a little luck, he might even become a leading actor like Richard Burbage or Edward Alleyn. Then playwrights would write plays to suit his special talents. Shakespeare, for example, wrote many of his tragedies with Richard Burbage in mind, and it was this actor who first rolled out the great speeches in *Hamlet, Othello* and *Macbeth.* And Christopher Marlowe wrote his masterpiece *Tamburlaine* for the famous actor Edward Alleyn.

Preparing a Play

When a playwright had written a play – and sometimes indeed before he had

30 (*Opposite top*) A performance of Thomas Kydd's *Spanish Tragedy*, written in 1589. This was the first of the popular tragedies in which a ghost called for revenge, and it is said to have inspired Shakespeare to write *Hamlet*. In this woodcut a boy actor is playing the part of the woman.

31 (*Left*) Edward Alleyn in a performance of *Dr Faustus*, 1636. This play, by Christopher Marlowe, tells of a man who sold his soul to the Devil in return for infinite knowledge.

32 The Earl of Essex, the proud favourite of Elizabeth I.

finished it – the company for whom he worked had copies of it produced, sometimes by hand, but increasingly on one of the new printing presses. Rehearsals began as soon as possible so that the company could add this new play to their stock, or repertory. Rehearsals were not the organized business which they have become in the modern theatre; there was little if any discipline about starting on time or listening to the producer. In *A Midsummer Night's Dream*, Shakespeare wrote a scene in which Bottom and his friends rehearse a play which they intend to put on. This comic scene may have been an exaggeration of what went on in real life – but may equally have been a fairly accurate reflection of the rehearsals which Shakespeare attended in Burbage's company.

While the rehearsals were going on, the producer was also attending to the costumes. Scenery was always very simple, but the costumes were usually rich and colourful – and costly. The cost was met out of the company's takings, and so lowered the profits that were shared out. Sometimes a company would buy costumes which a rich family were willing to sell. At other times an established company would sell its older costumes to a poor or a new company. Occasionally the beauty and worth of the costumes proved too great a temptation for one of the poorer paid members of the company, who would steal them to sell for some extra money. The costumes were always those of current fashion, so that Macbeth as well as Julius Caesar appeared in Elizabethan doublet and hose, although sometimes Julius Caesar might throw a piece of material across a shoulder in imitation of a Roman toga – a queer mixture of the ancient and modern.

While the rehearsals were going on and the costumes being made, the producer had also to look out for the equipment he needed for sound effects. In this he was following the tradition laid down by the miracle players. Fireworks, for example, were often used to simulate the sound of cannon-fire. In 1613, during a production of *Henry VIII* at the Globe Theatre, the producer used a real cannon as part of the sound effects which accompanied the glittering entry of Henry into his palace. Unfortunately, a piece of the smouldering wadding used in the cannon landed on the roof of the Globe and set light to the dry thatch. In a short time the famous theatre had burned to the ground – just three years before Shakespeare died in his native Stratford.

During the summer the London authorities insisted that the theatres should be closed in order to avoid the spread of the plague and other diseases. The acting companies then toured the major provincial towns and cities and earned money by putting on their old stock of plays.

The Influence of a Play

Some companies, as we have seen, only performed in the theatres once or twice a week – in the afternoons. On other days they put on special performances for the Queen or for noblemen friends of their patron. On one occasion this practice played a part in a rebellion against Elizabeth I. The Queen's favourite, the Earl of Essex, had returned from Ireland unsuccessful in his attempt to control the rebels. He had acted in Ireland as if he were a monarch himself, and back in London some of his friends persuaded him that he could well organize a rebellion against the ageing Queen. On 7 February 1601, Essex and his friends – including Lord Mounteagle, Sir Celli Meyrick and Sir Christopher Blount – commissioned a private performance of Shakespeare's *Richard II.* For this, the company was paid two pounds – a great sum of money in those days – and, in addition, was allowed to keep the admission money paid by others who came.

Richard II is the play in which Shakespeare depicted the successful overthrow of a reigning sovereign by the rebellious Henry Bolingbroke. After the play, Essex and his followers went back to Essex's home. When news of the gathering was brought to the Queen's Council, they feared that here were all the makings of an attempt at rebellion – a proud and defiant Essex, his swordsmen friends and their followers, and a play which taught men that it was right to overthrow a monarch. The Council sent a message to Essex that they wished to see him, but he refused to go. The Secretary, Herbert, then went in person to ask Essex to come before the Council. Essex and his friends, now at supper after their playgoing, realized that the Council had wind of their plot. The next day Essex rode against the Queen, but unlike his predecessor Bolingbroke he rode to defeat and death.

Changes in the Theatre

William Shakespeare died in 1616. But before his death, he had seen a change come over the theatrical scene. In 1609, for example, the playwright Dekker had written an article in which he advised the young man-about-town to misbehave in a playhouse. Dekker suggested the new type of play-goer should arrive late, clatter his stool on the stage, laugh during a tragedy, whistle during solemn moments and walk out if he were displeased.

The playhouses changed too. Shakespeare's later plays – such as *The Tempest* – were first performed in the new Blackfriars Theatre. This was small, warm and comfortable, and the first theatre in England to be roofed in. The interior was lit by candlelight and the stage was no longer the old apron stage of the open theatre. The Spaniards had been using painted and movable scenery for many years and the designer and architect Inigo Jones (*see* Chapter 7) had introduced the idea to England. But the painted scenery had to be disguised – the ends of the painted boards had to be hidden, and so had the ropes and pulleys which shifted the scenery. The easiest way to do this was to move the old archway from the back of the stage right to the front so that it stood in front of (or 'pro') the scenery. It was called the 'proscenium arch'. Each age has its drama – and the seventeenth century had a new stage as well.

33 Inside the Blackfriars Theatre. This still resembled the innyard theatres in some ways, but it was lit by candlelight and was much more comfortable. Notice too how most of the audience are kept away from the stage by a railing.

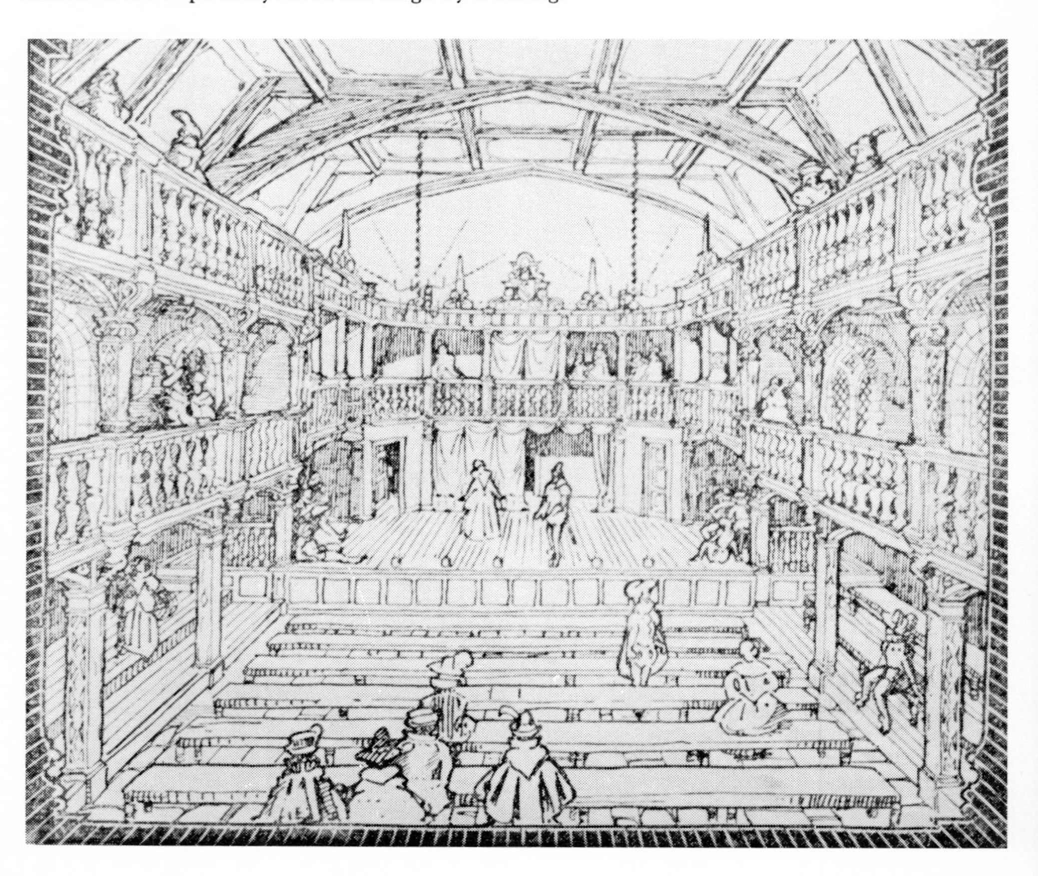

Chapter 7. The Theatre in the Seventeenth Century

Costly Theatres

In the old, open theatres such as the Globe, most of the audience had been standing and exposed to the weather. In the newer theatres, like the Blackfriars, people watched the plays in much greater comfort; the theatre was completely roofed in, there was seating of some sort for most of the audience and, with the advent of candlelighting, plays could be put on in the later afternoon or evening. In these new theatres the managers introduced the latest

34 The scenery designed by Inigo Jones for *Florimène*. Notice the use of perspective, which gives an impression of depth and distance.

fashion – the painted and movable scenery which Inigo Jones had brought back from his travels in Italy. Jones, the designer of the Banqueting Hall in Whitehall, also introduced the use of perspective in the painting of the new scenery.

All this was a far cry from the old theatres, with their apron stages jutting out into the audience and their lack of scenery. Now the stages had painted scenery at the back as well as along the sides, and a proscenium arch at the front. In effect, the actors now performed their plays in a sort of boxed-in room, which was artificially decorated and completely cut off from the audience.

The new theatres were much smaller than the old, open ones. While theatres had been open-roofed, there had been almost no limit to their size, and the Greeks and Romans had been able to build vast auditoriums. But when men decided to put a roof over the audience the builders were faced with a number of problems. They had to provide timbers for spanning the roof-space, cover these timbers with weatherproof material and decorate the inside of the new roof. These, and other problems, were more manageable if the space to be roofed-in was kept small. This helps to explain why the newer theatres built in the seventeenth century were, at first, much smaller than the old, open ones.

Because the new theatres were smaller, the audiences were of necessity also smaller. At the same time the expenses of running a theatre were going up and up. New and expensive scenery was being used, and new and expensive equipment was needed to move it. Theatre managers were forced to put up their admission prices, and as a result the groundlings, who had once formed the most important and largest section of the theatres' audiences, were now almost entirely excluded to make way for those who could afford to pay 10p and more for a seat.

The Masque

We have already seen that the more extreme Protestants, or Puritans, were opposed to the theatre even in Shakespeare's time. They may have associated theatre-going with the pagan rituals of maypoles and holy wells. But they probably had a point when they complained that the theatre was the scene of riotous and disorderly behaviour. And this was equally true of many performances of the masque – another Italian idea brought back to England by Inigo Jones.

The masque was essentially an after-dinner show put on at Court or in some nobleman's house to mark a special occasion. It consisted of a number of song-and-dance scenes, for which poets wrote special verses and songs. The most attractive part of the masque was the lavish costumes and scenery, which encouraged numbers of people to study scene designing and stagecraft. With its moveable scenery, splendid costume and singing, the masque was the forerunner of modern opera and ballet. But it did little to help playwrights or actors – everything was presented to the eye and little, if anything, left to the imagination of the audience. In addition, the masque was often accompanied by a great deal of misbehaviour. The following extract was written in 1607 by Sir John Harrington:

> After dinner the representation of Solomon in his temple, and the coming of the Queen of Sheba, was made, or as I may better say, was meant to have been made, before their Majesties, by the device of the Earl of Salisbury and others . . . The lady who did play the Queen's part did carry gifts to both their Majesties; but, forgetting the steps arising to the canopy, overset her casket into his Danish Majesty's lap, and fell at his feet . . . His Majesty then got up and would dance with the Queen of Sheba; but he fell down and humbled himself before her, and was carried into an inner chamber and laid on a bed of state; which was not a little defiled with presents of the queen which had been bestowed on his garments; such as wine, cream, jelly, beverage, cakes, spices and other good matters . . .

The Rule of the Puritans

The letter quoted above was written early in the reign of James I (1603-25). During the reign of his son Charles I (1625-49), the Civil War broke out, the King was executed, and for 18 years Britain was governed by the Puritans. Not surprisingly, one of the Puritans' first actions was to close down the theatres (in 1642), and to disband the licensed companies of actors. For 18 years there was no theatre in Britain – a dark age indeed.

Meanwhile, France had become the leading political power in Europe and it was the French writers and actors who now set the fashion. Famous French playwrights such as Molière, Corneille and Racine wrote a large number of plays, many of which are still performed – and, in translation, are part of the repertory of many British companies today. The French style of acting became widely admired and imitated. Dressed in the modern style, wearing the fashionable and huge wigs of the seventeenth century, the French actors marched around the stage until it was their turn to speak, when they advanced vigorously to the front of the stage, put hands on hips and roundly spoke their lines as if they were delivering a sermon. The actresses, on the other hand, wore the fashionable and huge hoops, mock jewellery and powdered hair, and minced their ways through the parts written for them.

The Restoration – of the Crown and the Theatre

In 1660 Charles II was restored to the British throne. Almost immediately he issued licences for two theatres to be opened in London. One licence went to William Davenant who was allowed to open a theatre at Covent Garden – an area which was being developed on plans designed by Inigo Jones. The other

AN

ORDINANCE
OF BOTH HOVSES OF PARLIAMENT.

For the ſuppreſſing of Publike Stage-Playes throughout the Kingdome, during theſe Calamitous Times.

Whereas the diſtreſſed Eſtate of Ireland, ſteeped in her own Blood, and the diſtracted Eſtate of England, threatned with a Cloud of Blood, by a Civill Warre; call for all poſſible meanes to appeaſe and avert the Wrath of God appearing in theſe Judgements: Amongſt which, Faſting and Prayer having bin often tryed to be very effectuall, have bin lately, and are ſtill enjoyned: And whereas publike Sports doe not well agree with publike Calamities, nor publike Stage-Playes with the Seaſons of Humiliation, this being an Exerciſe of ſad and pious Solemnity, and the other being Spectacles of Pleaſure, too commonly expreſſing lacivious Mirth and levitie: It is therfore thought fit, and Ordeined by the Lords and Commons in this Parliament Aſſembled, that while theſe ſad Cauſes and ſet times of Humiliation doe continue, publike Stage-playes ſhall ceaſe, and bee forborne. Inſtead of which, are recommended to the people of this Land, the profitable and ſeaſonable Conſiderations of Repentance, Reconciliation, and peace with God, which probably may produce outward peace and proſperity, and bring againe Times of Joy and Gladneſſe to theſe Nations.

Die Veneris, Septemb. *the* 2. 1642.

Ordered by the Lords and Commons Aſſembled in Parliament, that this Ordinance concerning Stage-Playes *be forthwith Printed and Publiſhed.*

John Browne Cler. Parliament.

Septemb. 3. London printed for Iohn Wright. 1642.

35 (*Above left*) A torchbearer in *The Masque of Blackness*, designed by Inigo Jones. Many of these costumes were covered in diamonds and other jewels.

36 (*Above right*) An ordinance published by the Puritan Parliament on 2 September 1642, in an attempt to close down all theatres.

licence was issued to Thomas Killigrew who opened his theatre in Drury Lane.

Both these theatres were roofed-in and were called 'private' theatres, unlike the open and 'public' theatres of Elizabethan London. Because of the cost of building, scenery and furnishing, the admission charge was always high, so that the audiences were composed largely of courtiers. The King and his immediate Court sat in front of the stage, and the rest of the audience in a semi-circle around them.

The two licensed theatres came under the supervision of the Lord Chamberlain. It was his duty to issue the licences, check that the conditions under which they were issued were kept, and see that when the original licensee died or retired the licence was sold to a suitable person. This control by the Lord Chamberlain was maintained for many years; until recently every play put

37 (*Above left*) Thomas Killigrew, to whom Charles II gave a patent to open a theatre in Drury Lane.

38 (*Above right*) An English actor imitates the artificial style of his French counterparts, advancing (on horseback) to the front of the stage to declaim his lines. 1697.

on in a theatre had to be officially approved; and dramatists and theatre managers often resented this form of censorship.

With the Restoration there was a rush by old actors and theatre managers to open up again. The terms under which the licences for London's two theatres had been issued forbade anyone else to open a theatre and charge the public an admission fee to see a play. But enterprising managers soon found a way around this. There was nothing, for example, to stop a man from opening a theatre and charging the public an admission fee to watch acrobats or jugglers, dancers or singers. And, once the public had paid to come into the theatre to see these variety shows, there was nothing to stop a company from putting on a play during the interval. In this way non-licensed theatres were opened in various parts of London and its suburbs.

Restoration Plays

Most of the plays written during the Restoration period are now considered bawdy and artificial. It seems as if playwrights and acting companies were trying to get their own back for the years of repression they had suffered under the Puritans. As one obscene play followed another, even the most outrageous of Charles II's courtiers got fed up and in 1682 only the Drury Lane Theatre remained open: Covent Garden was forced temporarily to close since it could not attract an audience.

Even the old classic plays were rewritten by the Restoration playwrights or managers. Davenant, for example, rewrote Shakespeare's *Measure for Measure* and *Much Ado about Nothing* to make his own *Law against Lovers* – in which he introduced singing, dancing and a chorus. *Macbeth* was treated in much the same way, and the witches flew across the stage singing pretty songs. *The Tempest* was turned into a spectacular but smutty comic opera, with music by Bannister. In one version of Shakespeare's *King Lear,* rewritten by Nahum Tate, a happy ending was thought to be essential. So King Lear was cured of his madness and regained his kingdom, while his two wicked daughters were poisoned – leaving Cordelia living happily ever after.

British Restoration actors imitated their French models – with their wigs and dress, and their stagy style of walking and speaking. One major new development was the appearance for the first time of actresses. In the past the parts of women had been played by men or boys. Now, actresses were allowed to appear on stage. This may be seen as a step in the direction of women's emancipation. But, for many people, it served merely as another proof that the stage and the theatre were hotbeds of evil-doing, where immoral men mixed with immoral women to produce immoral plays.

A number of actresses became very famous – none more so than Nell Gwynn. Charles II met Nell and another actress, Moll Davies, when the Court was at Tunbridge Wells in 1668. At first the King chose Moll Davies as his mistress, but after a short while he turned his attentions to Nell Gwynn. In the autumn of 1668, she retired from the stage to become Charles's favourite mistress. This was a great advance for the girl who had started her career serving at a bar in Drury Lane and later been an orange seller at the Drury Lane Theatre, before becoming an actress. She was greatly admired by many, including the diarist Samuel Pepys, who wrote of her part in John Dryden's *Maiden Queen*:

> But so great a performance of a comical part was never in the world before as Nell do this, both as a mad girl, then most and best of all when she comes in like a young gallant; and hath the motions and carriage of a spark the most that ever I saw any man have. It makes, me, I confess, admire her.

With a huge house in Pall Mall, and an income of £4,000 a year, Nell Gwynn

39 Mrs Bracegirdle – one of the first actresses to appear on the English stage – takes the leading role in *The Indian Queen*, which was written by the first woman playwright – G Aphra Behn.

could afford to give up the stage to become the mother of some of Charles's illegitimate children.

An Irishman to the Rescue

Not all playwrights, however, were willing to write bawdy scenes, nor to rewrite an old play. There were, for example, playwrights such as William Wycherley, William Congreve and George Farquhar who, by 1700, were introducing theatre-goers to good comedy and to plays about real life – one commentator described how they brought 'a breath of fresh country air into the mess that was the London theatre'.

But the English theatre was not really rescued from this mess until later in the eighteenth century, when an Irish dramatist – Richard Brindley Sheridan – wrote *The Rivals* and *The School for Scandal.* Almost two hundred years later another Irishman, George Bernard Shaw, performed a similar rescue.

Chapter 8. Between the Acts, 1737-1843

A New England

Between the Licensing Act of 1737 and the Theatre Act of 1843, Britain underwent a great change. In the early eighteenth century most people earned their living from farming, and lived in small towns or villages. Apart from London, the only towns of any size were Norwich and Bristol, with populations of about 30,000. Only London had purpose-built theatres, for no other town could provide a sufficiently large audience to support one.

By 1843, however, Britain was already 'the Workshop of the World'. Over half the population now lived in expanding towns or cities, many of which had populations of over 300,000. In these towns people worked in factories or

By His MAJESTY's COMPANY,
At the Theatre Royal in Drury-Lane,
This present MONDAY, May 27, 1776,
Will be presented a TRAGEDY, call'd
KING RICHARD the THIRD.
King Richard by Mr. GARRICK,
(Being his First Appearance in that Character these 4 Years)
Richmond by Mr. PALMER,
Buckingham by Mr. JEFFERSON,
Tressel by Mr. DAVIES,
Lord Stanley by Mr. BRANSBY,
Norfolk by Mr. HURST,
Catesby by Mr. PACKER,
Prince Edward by Miss P. HOPKINS,
Duke of York Master PULLEY, Lord Mayor Mr GRIFFITHS,
Ratcliffe by Mr. WRIGHT, Lieutenant by Mr. FAWCETT,
King Henry by Mr. REDDISH,
Lady Anne (First Time) Mrs. SIDDONS,
Dutchess of York by Mrs. JOHNSTON,
Queen by Mrs. HOPKINS.
To which will be added
The DEVIL to PAY.
Sir John Loverule by Mr. VERNON,
Jobson by Mr. MOODY,
Lady Loverule by Mrs. JOHNSTON,
Nell by Mrs. WRIGHTEN.
Ladies are desired to send their Servants a little after 5 to keep Places, to prevent Confusion.
The Doors will be opened at Half after FIVE o'Clock.
To begin exactly at Half after SIX o'Clock. Vivant Rex & Regina.
To-morrow, (by particular Desire) BRAGANZA, with Bon Ton, or High Life above Stairs.
(Being the last Time of performing them this Season.)
And Dancing by Mr. SLINGSBY and Signora PACINI.

40 (*Opposite*) Hogarth's 'Strolling Players', 1738, shows a company of actors rehearsing in a barn.

41 (*Above*) A playbill from the Theatre Royal, Drury Lane, informing the public that David Garrick will once again appear in the part of Richard III.

shipyards, cotton mills or coal mines, railway sheds or brickyards. There was an air of hustle and bustle as trains crossed the country on a network of lines, carrying people and goods at speeds approaching 50 mph.

A New Theatre

Each age has its own theatre, as we have seen, and in this period there were a number of developments which mark the age off from the past and point the way to the future. There were, for example, many new theatres built in the growing provincial towns. This is proof again that drama and the theatre is something natural to mankind; once enough well-to-do people had got their factories going, had built their homes and churches, their schools and hospitals, they turned to provide themselves with new methods of entertainment. Among other things, they built theatres and paid people to perform in them.

At first, in London, there were only the two licensed theatres – at Drury Lane and Covent Garden. As actors and managers saw that there was a demand for more theatres, many 'little' theatres were built. The Haymarket in London saw the opening of the Little, the Theatre Royal and the Queen's Theatre. There were also theatres at Sadler's Wells and in Lincoln's Inn Fields. These theatres were not licensed but they all presented plays and, until 1737, no one bothered about their unlicensed activities. In 1737, however, Henry Fielding produced a play at the Little Theatre in which he attacked the Prime Minister Robert Walpole. The government immediately rushed a Licensing Act through parliament to strengthen the law forbidding dramatic performances at any London theatres except the two patented ones. This Act also increased the power of the Lord Chamberlain to censor new plays.

However, the managers of the 'little' theatres got around the law by advertising concerts – for which they could charge a fee. Once the concert of music or dancing was over the audience then saw what they called 'a rehearsal for a play which we will not be able to put on in this house'.

While the government tried to limit the activities of dramatists, actors and managers in London, it did allow people to build theatres in some of the growing provincial towns – such as York, Bristol and Bath. These theatres were licensed so that the acting companies could then tour with their repertory of plays.

New Playwrights

Each age also produces its own dramatists, and in this respect the period 1737-1843 was reasonably fortunate. It saw two great playwrights – Oliver Goldsmith, whose most famous play is *She Stoops to Conquer,* and the Irishman Richard Brindley Sheridan. Unfortunately there were no others of outstanding ability, and most of the plays written in this period were poor comedies or even poorer melodramas such as those later described by Gustave Doré:

Next door to the Whitechapel Police Station, in Leman Street, is the Garrick Theatre. Gallery, one penny; pit, twopence; boxes, threepence. The pieces played at this establishment are, of course, adapted to the audience – the aristocrats among whom pay threepence for their seats. The first time we penetrated its gloomy passage, great excitement prevailed. The company were performing *The Starving Poor of Whitechapel*; and at the moment of our entry the stage policemen were getting very much the worst of a free fight, to the unbounded delight of pit and gallery . . . The drama was roughly performed. An infant prodigy . . . piped its lines of high-flown sentiment intelligently; the manager himself took the leading part in a broad, stagy sort of way, excellently well adapted to the audience – to judge from their applause; and everything was spiced highly to touch the tough palates of a Whitechapel audience. But in *The Starving Poor* comedy . . . the sentiments were worthy. Virtue is always rewarded in these humble dramatic temples; manly courage gets three times three; and woman is ever treated with respectful tenderness.

New Actors

The period 1737-1843 saw the rise of many great actors, and this had a major effect on the story of the theatre. Until 1737, people had mainly paid attention to the play itself or to the playwright. In Queen Elizabeth's time they had enjoyed *Macbeth* and in ancient Athens they had watched *Oedipus Rex*. People had been attracted to a new play because it was written by a playwright whose work they had already enjoyed.

But in the eighteenth century, for the first time, people began to follow the fortunes of a particular actor – and so the 'star system' was born. In the past the criticism and the praise had been heaped on the play or the playwright. Now the criticism and the blame were attached to the star actor; people began to know more about the stars than about the playwrights and their plays.

Indeed there was a galaxy of stars. There was Kean, Kemble and Macready and the female stars Fanny Kemble and Sarah Siddons. But above all there was David Garrick (1717-79), who has been called the father of his profession and after whom is named not only a great theatre, but also a club for actors and actresses. Garrick brought a new style of acting to the notice of the public, and made it so popular that other actors had to follow his example. This was the end of the false and mannered style that actors had learned from the French.

Garrick was not in fact the first to adopt this new style, which was based on a faithful study of real people. Charles Macklin was an established actor before Garrick even appeared on the stage. On 14 March 1741 Macklin arrived at Drury Lane to play Shylock, in an adaptation of Shakespeare's famous play *The Merchant of Venice*. This adaptation by Lord Lansdowne had first appeared in 1701 and in it the noble lord had turned Shylock into a comic character. Macklin was determined to play the part as he thought Shakespeare had meant it to be played. He put on heavy make-up to make his face appear very lined and worn; he wore a beard, a red hat and a black cloak. All this was the result of research he had done; from his reading, he believed it to be the way Venetian Jews dressed in Shakespeare's time. Macklin himself has described how, when it was his turn to appear on the stage:

> My heart began to beat. However I mustered all the courage I could and, recommending my cause to Providence, threw myself boldly on the stage, and was received by one of the loudest thunders of applause I ever before experienced.

This was the first time that the audience had seen the part played in this way. At first they were astonished and then, as Macklin wrote, people began to murmur: 'Very well – very well indeed! This man seems to know what he is about.' By the end of the play the manager was so delighted with the applause that he came out in person to congratulate Macklin.

George II had watched the performance from the Royal Box. On the following morning, so we are told:

> . . . at a Prime Minister's audience with his sovereign, Sir Robert Walpole said, 'I wish, your Majesty, it was possible to find a recipe for frightening the House of Commons!' 'Vat you tink,' asked George II, who confessed to a sleepless night, 'of sending dem to see dat Irishman play Shylock?'

David Garrick's First Appearance

Garrick had had some minor success in unlicensed theatres as an actor in the old, French school when he was invited to play in an unlicensed theatre on 19 October 1741, some time after Macklin's success as Shylock. The playbill reads:

42 Charles Macklin (with beard) in the part of Shylock in *The Merchant of Venice*. Notice the eighteenth-century idea of the way Venetian Jews dressed in Shakespeare's time.

43 David Garrick's portrayal of Richard III. This performance won Garrick great fame and persuaded other actors to be more realistic in their roles.

At the late Theatre in Goodman's fields, this day, will be performed
a Concert of Vocal and Instrumental Music, divided into Two Parts
Tickets at three, two and one shilling.
Places for Boxes to be taken at The Fleece
Tavern, next the Theatre.
NB. Between the two parts of the Concert will be presented an
Historical Play, called
The life and Death of
King Richard the Third
Containing the distress of K.Henry VI.
The artful acquisition of the Crown
by King Richard
The murder of young King Edward V. and
his brother in the Tower
The landing of the Earl of Richmond: and the death of
King Richard in the memorable battle of Bosworth-field;
being the last that was fought between the houses of
York and Lancaster.
With many other true Historical passages.
The part of King Richard by a Gentleman (who
never appeared on
any stage).

It is not true that Garrick had never appeared on any stage, but it was true that this was his first appearance in London in a leading part. Notice too how the unlicensed theatres got round the problem of not being allowed to charge for admission to a play. London audiences had seen other actors peform the part of Richard III. Like many of Shakespeare's works, this play had also been adapted in the seventeenth century. Audiences were used to hearing an orchestra play introductory music and then seeing an actor strut about the stage, reciting in a sing-song voice and with exaggerated gestures, indicating that 'now I am depressed' or 'now I am in a temper'.

Macklin was present when Garrick made his appearance as Richard. He wrote:

> The character he assumed was visible in his countenance; the power of his imagination was such that he transformed himself into the very man; the passions rose in rapid succession, and before he uttered a word, were legible on every feature of that various face . . . The rage and rapidity with which he spoke:
>
> *The North! what do they in the North?*
> *When they should serve their Sovereign in the West?*
>
> made a most astonishing impression. His soliloquy in the tent scene discovered the inward man. Everything he described was almost reality; the spectator thought he heard the hum of either army from camp to camp, and steed threatening steed. When he started from his dream he was a spectacle of horror. He called out in a manly tone: *Give me another horse!*

The audience had never seen such a Richard – such evil in his voice, such passion in the love scene with Lady Anne. They shouted their approval at this new, natural style of acting. The next morning the *Daily Post* noted:

> Last night, was performed gratis the tragedy of *King Richard the Third* at the late theatre in Goodman's Fields, when the character of Richard was performed by a gentleman who never appeared before, whose reception was the most extraordinary and great that was ever known on such an occasion. We hear he obliges the town this evening with the same performance.

The playwright Sheridan thought Garrick's performance was 'fine but not terrible enough', to which Mrs Siddons – who had played Lady Anne – replied, 'God bless me! What could be more terrible?' Garrick himself said towards the end of his career: 'I gained my fame by Richard and mean to end by it'. On 7 June 1776 he gave a Royal Command performance as Richard III. On 10 June he announced his retirement.

44 (*Above*) A painting by H Fuseli of Mrs Siddons as Lady Macbeth.

45 (*Right*) The pit entrance at Drury Lane in October 1784. Women lose their hats and shoes, men lose their wigs, and everyone pushes and shoves in the struggle to get a seat.

46 'Hooliganism' at Covent Garden Theatre in 1809 in support of a demand for 'old prices'. The theatre was often the scene of riots by patrons, either demanding a reduction in prices or reacting against the performance of a particular actor.

The Audience

The managements of the licensed theatres were quick to realize Garrick's potential. Vast crowds of fashionable people jostled to see his performances. Lords and ladies would send their servants round to the theatre at three o'clock in the afternoon to book seats, and then, come the evening, would crowd forth in their sedan chairs and chaises. The streets around the theatre quickly became full of vehicles and bearers, waiting for the rich patrons of the theatre to come out. Inside, the audience had the benefit of the covered roof and the spectacle of the expensive machinery – although the more observant would have noticed that the same scenery was used time and again. Beneath the same balcony they saw Shylock in one play and Romeo in another; in the same parlour many different scenes were acted; the blasted heath on which the witches met Macbeth was also used for Bosworth Field and the cliffs of Dover.

Some of the audience were allowed their seats on the stage – paying the exorbitant price of 50p for the privilege. Others crowded along the sides of the stage so that they too had 'a place among the scenes'.

Audiences in those days were not as well behaved as they are today. Indeed, reports of their behaviour would indicate that it was rather like the hooliganism that now takes place at some football matches. On 14 December 1702 a Mr Goodyer and a Mr Fielding – who had bought highly priced seats on the stage – drew their swords and engaged in a duel while a play was going on; and it was quite common for actors to be pelted with eggs or fruit or sometimes even with bottles. One report reads:

> Thursday night there was a great riot at Covent Garden playhouse, without the least plea or pretence whatever, occasioned by the gentry in the upper gallery calling for a hornpipe, though nothing of the sort was expressed in the bills. They went so far as to throw a quart bottle and two pint bottles upon the stage, which happily did no mischief, but might have been productive of a great deal.

To try to avoid this sort of trouble many playwrights invited their friends to come along to their plays, so that no room was left for troublemakers. A popular star actor, one whom audiences wanted to hear, was also of benefit to the theatre managers and playwrights. But even the stars could be attacked by an audience. Sometimes the supporters of one star – perhaps of Edmund Kean or Charles Kemble – would go to the theatre where another star, Garrick for instance, was appearing, merely to make trouble. Sometimes an otherwise friendly audience would be roused against even a popular actor because of the way in which he dealt with the play. There was, by the mid-eighteenth century, a traditional way of acting certain parts in the well-known Shakespearean plays. If an actor or actress tried to play the part in any other way, the audience often reacted violently. Macklin and Garrick had educated audiences to accept a more realistic treatment of certain Shakespearean parts. But even Garrick was horrified when he heard that Sarah Siddons was going to alter the way in which the part of Lady Macbeth was traditionally played. Mrs Siddons had decided that, in the sleep walking scene, she would put down the candle she was carrying in order to give more strength to the lines where Lady Macbeth talks about washing her hands clean of blood. Despite Garrick's advice, Mrs Siddons went ahead with her new way of playing the part. The actor-manager, Sheridan, thought the new interpretation successful; yet others criticized the great star for breaking with tradition.

There was also a traditional way of dressing for a particular part. On one occasion, Garrick tried to show that Macbeth was upset by leaving undone the buttons of his waistcoat. The audience was incensed, and booed and shouted at him for being so careless of tradition. When Macklin played the part of Macbeth, he dressed up in what were then considered tartans – but the rest of the cast still wore the court dress of the eighteenth century with wigs and expensive shoes. And Sarah Siddons was considered to be very daring, because she left off the fashionable hoop and wig in order to be able to move more freely around the stage.

Family Opposition

Garrick's first job had been as a partner, with his brother Peter, in the wine

47 Edmund Kean plays the part of Richard III at Drury Lane in 1820. In the Royal Box are the Duke of York, the Prince Regent (later George IV) and the Duke of Wellington. The theatre was still popular with the Court and upper classes, and the middle class had begun to follow their example.

trade. He had kept his ambition to be an actor a secret, but his success in *Richard III* meant that his family would soon know about it – and feel betrayed by his course of action. So in October 1741 he wrote to his uncle:

Dear Sir,

I suppose you must have heard by this time of my playing King Richard at Goodman's Fields, and I suppose you are apprehensive I design to continue on the stage.

You must know that since I have been in business (the Wine Trade, I mean), I have run out almost half of my fortune, and tho' to this day I don't owe anything, yet the terrible prospect of running it all out made me think of something to redeem it. My mind led me to the stage, which from being very young I found myself inducing to, and have been very unhappy that I could not come upon it before. The only thing that gives me pain is that my friends, I suppose, will look very cool upon me . . . But what can I do? I am wholly bent upon the thing, and can make £300 per annum out of it. As my brother will settle at Litchfield, I design to throw up the Wine Business as soon as I can conveniently . . . If you should want to speak with me, the Stage Door will always be open to you, or any other part of the house, for I am Manager with Mr Giffard – and you may always command

Yr most humble servant
D Garrick

Although his family were not convinced he had done the right thing, Garrick's star was to go on shining for many years, earning for the actor a huge income – on average over £500 a year, which was a vast sum of money at that time – and winning for him hundreds of 'fans'. But to earn this money and to keep the support of the fans was hard work. There was no tradition of a long-running play in those days. Garrick performed *Richard III* one night and then might not play it again for a week or two; in the meantime he might play in three or four other productions. Sometimes he acted in two plays in one evening – like when he played the old, mad King Lear followed by a performance as a 15-year-old boy in Collie Cibber's play *The Schoolboy of the Comical Rival.* As Lear he was very successful – the audience, we are told, sobbed. Many years later he explained how he had learned to play the part of Lear. He knew of a man who had accidentally killed his own daughter by dropping her from a window. He had become mad, but being fairly well-off he had been allowed to remain at home, where he was guarded by two keepers supervised by his doctor. Garrick, who wanted to know how Lear would feel after killing a daughter, went to this house and studied the actions of the poor father. He watched while the madman imagined that he was playing with his dead daughter. 'There it was', said Garrick, 'that I learned to imitate madness; I copied nature and to that owed my success in *King Lear*.'

Rivalry and Bad Behaviour

There were a number of other stars with their own loyal followers, and enough money to recruit people to sit in the cheap seats and applaud their favourites. Sometimes ruffians were employed to make life uncomfortable for a rival star, and riotous behaviour was common in London theatres. In 1782, C P Moritz wrote in his book *Travels in England*:

> Besides this perpetual pelting from the gallery, which renders an English playhouse so uncomfortable, there is no end to their calling out and knocking with their sticks till the curtain is drawn up. I saw a miller's boy, like a huge booby, leaning over the rails and knocking again and again on the outside with all his might, so he was seen by everybody, without being in the least ashamed or abashed. I sometimes heard too the people in the lower or middle gallery quarrelling with those in the upper one. Behind me in the pit, sat a young fop, who in order to display his costly stone-buckles with utmost brilliancy, continually put his foot on my bench, and even sometimes upon my coat . . .

Despite the improved acting and the revived interest in drama, the theatre in the eighteenth century remained a very uncouth and rough affair.

Chapter 9. The Victorian Theatre

The Spirit of the Age

By the time Queen Victoria came to the throne in 1837, Britain had already undergone a great deal of industrial change. This was producing a new class of rich merchants, factory and mine owners, bankers and professional people such as lawyers, engineers, doctors and accountants. By 1914, when the First World War broke out, this middle class had transformed Britain into a modern industrial state, won an Empire 'on which the sun never set', and in the process made themselves extremely wealthy.

It was this rich, confident, conquering and successful middle class that created the spirit of the age. We know a little of that spirit from the many proverbs left to us. 'Look after the pennies and the pounds will look after themselves' and 'Waste not, want not' are two proverbs which Victorians invented to help teach their children and servants the virtue of thrift; and 'Cleanliness is next to Godliness' was one by which they hoped to teach the poor some good habits. They themselves, of course, had also to be taught good habits. Mrs Isabella Beeton wrote her *Book of Household Management* to help wives successfully to run their homes with armies of servants; and in 1898 Mrs C E Humphrey wrote *Manners for Men* in which we read:

> It is a piece of bad manners to enter the theatre late, disturbing the audience and annoying the players or singers. It is equally rude to leave before the entertainment is ended, unless the interval be chosen when nothing is going on.
>
> Between the acts of a play the modern man thinks it his duty to himself to go out and have a drink and perhaps smoke a cigarette. But who shall say what golden opinions are won by those who refrain from acquiring the odour of tobacco, or whisky, while they are in the company of ladies in the

48 A stage play licence, dated 7 July 1849, issued by the Lord Chamberlain to the Manager of the Britannia Inn, Hoxton, allowing the performance of a drama in two acts entitled *Robert Ryland* or *The Carpenter's Family*.

July 7th 1849.

It having been represented to Me by the Examiner of All Theatrical Entertainments that a Manuscript entituled "Robert Ryland," or "The Carpenter's family," being a drama in two Acts ——

does not in its general tendency contain any thing immoral or otherwise improper for the Stage I The Lord Chamberlain of Her Majesty's Household do by virtue of my Office and in pursuance of the Act of Parliament in that case provided Allow the Performance of the said Manuscript ——
at your Salon, with the exception of all Words and Passages which are specified by the Examiner in the endorsement of this License and without any further variations whatsoever.

Breadalbane

To The Manager of the
Britannia Salon

49 (*Below*) One of the first performances at the Holborn Theatre, London, 13 October 1866. The house is well-lit and the fashionable audience is wearing full evening dress. This and other new theatres were cleaner, more comfortable and better ventilated than the old theatres had been – and admission charges were correspondingly higher.

heated atmosphere of a theatre?

Apart from the lady he is with and considerations connected with her, there is the inconvenience to which many of the audience are subjected by the passing in and out of so many. However, it is a recognized custom, so much so that a smoking foyer is attached to all the best theatres, and a warning bell is rung in it by the management a few minutes before the rising of the curtain.

Refreshments are frequently carried round by attendants to private boxes, and sometimes in the stalls as well. Should they appear, it is the duty of the gentleman of the party to ask the ladies if they wish for any, and to pay for what is consumed. It is, however, a rare thing for ladies to eat or drink at the play.

The gentleman also pays for the programme at the few theatres where a charge is made.

The Theatres

Mrs Humphrey's advice was needed because theatre-going had become an almost essential part of the life of the Victorian middle class. In 1837 there were 22 theatres in London, but only two of them were licensed; the others, as we have seen in Chapter 8, had to put on plays during the interval between variety acts. In 1843, a new Theatre Act allowed the opening of theatres under licence from the Lord Chamberlain provided that there was no selling of food and no smoking in the theatre. This had two effects: it encouraged some people to open new theatres, but at the same time discouraged the managers of unlicensed theatres, who depended on the sale of food and drink to make a profit. Many of these decided not to apply for a theatrical licence but instead to turn their buildings into music halls, where only variety turns would be shown.

After 1843, taking advantage of the Theatre Act, a number of new theatres were opened in London and in the growing industrial towns. These theatres also took advantage of the increased skills of British designers and builders, inventors and furniture makers – they were larger, more comfortable, better lit and better furnished than the old theatres had been.

Managers also tried to make their theatres attractive to their customers by employing artists to produce beautiful but expensive scenery, with advanced machinery to move it on and off the stage. Dramatists began to write plays which demanded a great deal of scenery and producers became used to having this available at the theatre.

Actors earned very high salaries – as Garrick and others had done – so that the cost of putting on a play spiralled. As a result many managers increased seat prices to the point where only the rich could afford them. The less well-off rarely, if ever, went to the fashionable theatres.

50 (*Top*) A playbill for a 'well-made' melodrama – with the villain (in the right-hand corner), the swooning heroine (in the centre), and the emphasis on virtue triumphing over evil (in the poem in the left-hand corner).

51 Sir Herbert Tree in *Twelfth Night*, during a visit to Berlin in 1907. Notice the realism of the stage setting – real grass, real bushes and correct Elizabethan dress.

52 (*Above left*) An advertisement for a play at the Theatre Royal, South Shields, in June 1907. The villain is about to marry the heroine against her will, when the hero comes dashing to the rescue.

53 (*Above right*) A scene from a performance of George Bernard Shaw's *Pygmalion* at His Majesty's Theatre, April 1914, with Mrs Patrick Campbell (*left*) as the outspoken Eliza Doolittle.

In these expensive theatres managers provided the rich with a numbered seat which could be booked in advance, and presented plays which they hoped would attract an audience from the wealthy middle class. What sort of play do you think would appeal to them? Remember that by now a visit to a theatre had become 'an event', even for the middle class. It was no longer thought fit to go to the theatre as casually as one now goes to the cinema. In Victorian Britain a visit to the theatre was increasingly regarded as part of 'an evening out'; people dressed up, had a meal in a restaurant, and then at about 8 o'clock went on to the theatre.

Such patrons did not want to watch 'a problem play', in which some dramatist tried to work out one or other of the many social problems of the day. They much preferred to watch a well-known play, a revival of Shakespeare perhaps, or a play by a well-known Victorian dramatist – a play which showed that virtue will always overcome vice, that the honest are always rewarded, and that good men are always 'nice' to women who in turn are fair, weak and helpless. In such melodramas the presence of a well-known star actor in the main part was enough to guarantee a full house – and a profit for the management which had laid out large sums of money to build, equip and furnish the theatre.

Even the very well-off had to take note of the price of a visit to the theatre. Writing in the *Cornhill Magazine* in June 1901, G Colmore addressed an article to people whose income was large enough to allow them to employ four servants. For these people he wrote:

> Playgoing must be strictly limited, for theatre and music-hall tickets run away with a lot of money, and there is always the expense of the journey hither and thither. The real lovers of music can indulge their taste at very little cost. On the whole it comes to this, that a pretty home, comfortably kept, and an easy mind, unshaken by the thought of the Christmas bills, are better worth having than a large acquaintance, much entertaining, and many amusements; and that for most people who live on eight hundred a year these things are not compatible.

How unlike the people's theatre of Shakespeare's England!

Long Runs

In Chapter 8 we saw how David Garrick acted many different parts in a very short space of time – playing, for example, 119 characters in different plays within the space of six months. This was the traditional life of the actor, who was expected to build up a repertoire of parts to which he constantly added, either by learning parts in old plays or by learning new plays as they appeared. The repertory companies, like those to which Garrick belonged, put on a different play each night, and maybe even two plays on some nights. But in the Victorian theatres this custom died out, and the new practice of the long run was started. This has now become a tradition, and it is easy to understand why when you consider the cost of scenery for a play, the star's salary and the higher salaries required by all the supporting actors. This meant that the expense of putting on a play was much greater than it had ever been – and no theatre could afford to put on a different play, with expensive scenery and elaborate costumes, every night.

This also helps to explain the nature of the plays written by Victorian dramatists. Theatre managers knew that if they had a star actor or actress in a leading role they could fill a theatre for a long run with, for example, a revival of a Shakespeare play. In 1874 Sir Henry Irving played Hamlet on 200 nights, and no doubt made a profit for the theatre owners as well as earning a high salary for himself. When a Victorian dramatist brought a new play to a theatre owner or manager, the first question in the mind of the owner was: 'Will the patrons come to watch this for the next twelve months?' If he thought they would not, then he refused the play; and since the Victorian middle class showed that they liked melodrama in which the hero won and the villain was conquered, that was the sort of play which Victorian dramatists were persuaded to write. Each age, indeed, has its own theatre.

New Plays, 1900-14

The managers and actors who wanted the expensive scenery argued that they were seeking a greater realism in their work. If the play was supposed to be set in an eighteenth-century drawing room then, they said, everything in the set had to be exactly right – eighteenth-century clocks, carpets, chairs, clothes and so on. No more, for them, the simple painted backcloth of Garrick's day; even less the plain theatre of Elizabethan England. This, they declared, was realism.

But at the same time their new plays were far from being realistic or true to life. They were, in fact, plays in which wicked squires left swooning girls to die in front of a roaring train, only for the dashing hero to sweep the damsel to safety while on his way to punish the cowardly fleeing villain. Realistic indeed! There were very few, if any, plays which were concerned with the real lives of ordinary people in nineteenth-century Britain.

Around 1900, however, a new spirit began to emerge – a spirit of enquiry into current social problems. People such as Charles Booth and Seebohm Rowntree carried out massive research which showed that about one-third of the people in Britain lived in dire poverty. There was also a new spirit of militancy – by women, for example, who began to demand equal rights with men. Even the politicians were affected by this new spirit, and laws were passed concerning health, unemployment, school medical inspection and school meals – all of which indicated that the government was at last willing to play an active role in the lives of ordinary people.

Not surprisingly, this new spirit produced a new theatre. Henrik Ibsen (1828-1906) was a Norwegian who wrote plays dealing with the most serious issues of the time. In Britain, his example was followed by George Bernard Shaw. Shaw was a member of the socialist Fabian Society, and had been largely responsible for the successful link-up between the various socialist societies and the trade union movement which in 1900 created the Labour Party. He was deeply involved both enquiring into contemporary problems and endeavouring to find solutions, and his plays reflect his social concern. He wrote about poverty, for example, and the rights of women, the problems of war and pacifism, the rights of coloured people. He was also endowed with a great sense of humour so that his plays are enjoyable as well as being committed. To Shaw we owe the modern social drama in which a playwright examines some current

54 (*Opposite*) Charles Kean plays Richard II at the Princess' Theatre. Charles did not have the ability of his father, but he enjoyed the freedom of improved stage design, and splendid scenery added to the atmosphere of the play.

and very real problem. Shaw was the first English-speaking dramatist to take this line, and in so doing he rescued the theatre from the trough into which it had fallen during Queen Victoria's reign. Shaw, like Sheridan (*see* Chapter 7) was an Irishman, and proudly announced this fact in his play *John Bull's Other Island*.

Victorian Actors

At the beginning of the nineteenth century a new star began to dominate the London theatres. Edmund Kean (1787-1833) showed that a natural and yet passionate method of acting was both effective and popular. The poet Samuel Coleridge wrote: 'To see Kean act was to read Shakespeare by flashes of lightning'. Lord Byron admitted that he had been frightened out of his life while watching Kean play the part of Overreach in *A New Way to Pay Old Debts*. 'All over the house women screamed and fainted' – indeed, even the principal actress, Mrs Glover, passed out from the excitement. It is not surprising then to read in a newspaper account of the performance that the audience stood clapping and 'giving him an ovation such as Drury Lane had never seen'.

Edmund Kean's son, Charles (1811-68), carried on this natural style of acting, vying with his great rival Macready. Charles Kean and Macready were actor-managers, controlling both the theatres in which they appeared and the companies employed in those theatres. One result of their position was the further development of the star system; they ensured that only their parts were of any importance, and insisted that even Shakespeare's plays were remoulded to suit them. One writer, referring to Macready, notes:

> When he played Othello, Iago was to be *nowhere*. Iago was to be a mere stroller whose business was to supply Othello's passion with fuel and keep up his high-pressure. The next night, perhaps, he took Iago and then everything was changed. Othello was to be a mere puppet for Iago to play with.

Not only were the old classical plays rewritten. New plays were also chosen solely because they provided a large part for the actor-manager – or were rejected because the part of the male lead was not considered important enough. Since the plays that were put on centred inevitably on the one star, there was little if any need for rehearsals. The rest of the cast had only to know how to feed the star with his cues. The star remained at the centre of the stage with the spotlight (called 'the limelight') focussed on him alone. No young actor would ever dare try to steal the limelight from an established star.

The end of the nineteenth century saw the most famous actor-manager become established as the popular favourite. This was Henry Irving (1838-1905), who took over the Lyceum Theatre and was partnered by the equally brilliant and beautiful Ellen Terry. In 1895 Irving received a knighthood from Queen Victoria and, as Sir Henry, continued to act until his death in 1905. This royal recognition of the acting profession did much to make it respectable in the eyes of the loyal middle classes.

Learning to Act

Another famous actor, Herbert Beerbohm Tree (1852-1917), was also given a knighthood. It was Tree who realized that actors had to be better prepared for their profession than they had been, and he was largely responsible for setting up the Royal Academy of Dramatic Art (RADA), to which aspiring actors and actresses can go to learn the rudiments of their profession – how to speak properly, how to play different characters and how to perform certain actions realistically – such as falling down, dying, being happy or sad. In the past, actors had either learned these things for themselves (as Garrick did), or they had not bothered and had spoiled many plays by their clumsy acting.

In 1898 a Russian, Stanislavski, founded the Moscow Arts Theatre because he was dissatisfied with the artificial style of acting in Russia – where they still modelled themselves on the eighteenth-century French style. Stanislavski taught his pupils that if they wished to act a certain part they had first to 'become' the character. This 'method' is now followed by many acting schools and academies, although the potential actor still has to learn the basic principles taught at the more traditional schools such as RADA.

By the end of the nineteenth century, acting and the theatre were well established as a profession.

Chapter 10. The Theatre in a Changing World, 1900 - 1939

Revivals and Escapism

At the beginning of this century, Britain was shattered by the horrors of the First World War (1914-18), when literally millions of men were killed or seriously wounded. It is difficult for us today to imagine the grief and suffering in homes where fathers, husbands and brothers were victims of the 'war to end all wars'. It is equally difficult for us, looking back, to imagine the shattering effect that the war had on people who had been brought up to believe that the world was constantly improving, that men would continue forever to conquer

55 Noel Coward and Gertrude Lawrence star in Coward's *Private Lives*, 1930. Middle-class theatre-goers flocked to see such plays as an escape from the harsh realities of world depression and the threat of war.

56 A scene from a 1936 production of *Murder in the Cathedral*, by T S Eliot.

more and more of nature, until one day, like the title of a book written at the time, *Men Will Be Like Gods*.

The war proved that modern man was capable of inflicting great suffering on his fellow men. After it there were very few who shared the confidence once expressed by H G Wells and others concerning the glorious future that awaited liberated mankind. A far greater number of men realized that it would be: 'Never glad, confident morning again'.

In this situation, many people reacted by trying to get as much fun out of life as possible. 'The gay twenties' were enjoyed by fashionable people seeking their pleasure in the new jazz clubs, night clubs – and theatres. To satisfy these new demands, managers made their theatres and stages more glittering than they had ever been – to help their patrons escape from the harsh realities of the post-war world with its unemployment, industrial unrest and threats of more wars to come. Dramatists, too, wrote pleasant, light and frothy plays in which rich young people enjoyed a wonderfully humorous, pleasant – and unreal – life.

However, there were a number of playwrights who produced more serious works. George Bernard Shaw continued to write plays in which he posed, and answered, questions of social and political importance, as did J B Priestley, a Yorkshireman. Sean O'Casey, a Catholic Irish playwright, used his plays to attack the role of the Church in Ireland. *Juno and the Paycock* and *The Plough and the Stars* are two of his plays which could be seen in London although they were banned in Ireland. An American dramatist, Eugene O'Neill, wrote rather gloomy plays in which the characters criticize widely held conventional views, and suggest that all is not well with the world.

Another American playwright, T S Eliot, wrote *Murder in the Cathedral* which had its first production in the chapter house of Canterbury Cathedral, where Thomas Becket was supposed to have been murdered. Eliot's play was unusual not only in its theme – the murder of the Archbishop – but also in its setting – a cathedral. It was even more unusual in that Eliot wrote his play as a verse drama – as Shakespeare had done. But perhaps the most unusual thing about this play was Eliot's use of the women of Canterbury, who spoke his poetry rather in the way that the Greek chorus (*see* Chapter 2) had spoken the words of the earliest playwrights.

Stage Designers

The actor-managers of the late nineteenth century had insisted on 'realism' in their stage sets and scenery. After the First World War, an increasing number of designers were influenced by the work of Gordon Craig – the son of Ellen Terry – whose sets avoided fussy, over-realistic details and instead had actors performing on different levels, where they were picked out by suitably placed spot lighting.

These new designers were employed by a small group of stage directors – the men who see a play through all its stages from first reading to final production. One of the features of the theatre in this century has been the increasingly important part played by directors. They have, in many cases, been the 'new stars', so that people are attracted to a particular play specifically because it is directed by Peter Hall or some other outstanding director. These 'new men' welcomed the change in stage design, because it freed the play from concern for unimportant detail and threw everyone's attention back on the actors, the words, and the play itself.

Experiment

The new playwrights and new directors were willing to experiment in a number of ways. They insisted that their actors should perform as naturally as possible – not declaiming their lines as some of the actor-managers had done, nor speaking too slowly. This had become a bad habit with many actors and one had taken over six minutes to recite the famous soliloquy from *Hamlet* which begins 'To be or not to be'! Lilian Baylis at the Old Vic and Barry Jackson at the Kingsway Theatre were two of the directors who insisted that the actor should not interfere between the playwright and the audience, but should let the play speak for itself. They urged actors to stand, walk, lounge, sit down, yawn and do all the things that ordinary people do as naturally as possible. Barry Jackson took his ideas a step further when, in 1925, he staged a

57 Laurence Olivier as Henry V in an Old Vic production of the Shakespeare play, 1937.

58 (*Below*) A music hall which provided live entertainment as well as modern 'pictures'. On the left the clock shows the time of the next performance, and in the centre you can see the price of admission – three old pence.

performance of *Hamlet* in modern dress. Many people were outraged at this break with the convention grown up in the nineteenth century. They had forgotten that Shakespeare's players had worn Elizabethan dress, and that the great stars of the eighteenth century – Garrick, Siddons, Kemble and others – had worn the contemporary court dress.

Amateur Dramatics

We have already seen how the poorer people drifted away from the theatre in the late nineteenth century as admission charges went up, and turned instead to music halls and cheaper theatres. It was in these theatres that the first moving films were shown. In the late 1920s, when the film became 'the talking picture', many of these older theatres and music halls were converted into cinemas.

One of the mainstays of the Victorian theatre died out as the strolling groups which had once toured the country were forced to disband. Not enough people were willing to pay to see them perform, and most audiences would rather watch the new stars of the silver screen, and the more lavish cinema productions. In one town after another repertory companies were dissolved as theatre owners pulled down their stages to make way for the screens needed for the new films, or sold their sites and watched the buildings being pulled down to make way for some modern development.

However, almost paradoxically, there was at the same time a tremendous growth in the numbers of those taking part in amateur dramatics. In the past, people had been content to be merely a passive audience during a play. Now, in the 1930s, as the chances of ever being an audience at a live theatrical show dwindled, the new generation began to take on a major role in the production of a play, by becoming the actors themselves. In the nineteenth century their grandparents had sat open-mouthed watching strolling players as they performed some melodrama or other. More educated than their grandparents, the young now went on to the stage themselves. In church halls and small cinemas, in the local school hall or in the halls attached to working men's clubs – anywhere, in fact, where they could seat an audience – local drama groups were formed, which presented plays for their friends and neighbours, and for their own enjoyment.

To help promote this new interest in the theatre the British Drama League was formed. Drama groups could borrow scripts from the League's Library, which also offered advice and practical guidance. The League ran training courses for people whose only ambition might be to direct or produce a play in a local church hall. Competitive festivals were organized to encourage local groups and to keep alive the theatre as it struggled against growing competition from the cinema and the economic depression of the 1930s.

Chapter 11. The Theatre Today

The War and the Theatre, 1939-45

During the Second World War (1939-45) the government felt it was in the national interest to encourage the professional theatre. They believed that British workers and their families, as well as members of the armed forces, needed a boost to their morale – which the theatre could provide. Companies of actors were set up to tour the country and make overseas visits, performing their plays before both civilians and troops. With limited opportunities for entertainment and with more money than they could spend on food, clothes and other rationed goods, people flocked to see these shows. In London the theatres played before packed houses.

Television and the Theatre in the 1950s

However, this boom was short-lived. With the return to normal conditions – the end of rationing, the opening of holiday camps and the freedom to take holidays abroad – families found that they had more opportunities for entertainment than they had enjoyed during the war. In particular, the British copied the American example and became avid watchers of television. People no longer had to leave their homes in search of entertainment, but could sit back in comfort and watch it on the box. Thousands of cinemas closed down because of lack of audiences, and throughout the country many provincial repertory companies also closed. In London the theatre carried on, partly owing to the large number of overseas tourists for whom a visit to a London theatre was part of their annual vacation, and partly owing to the many provincial people who could afford to come to London for a day and a night out, including a visit to a theatre.

To attract these passing audiences the London theatres imported American musical shows – such as *Oklahoma*, *Annie Get Your Gun* and *The Sound of*

59 Entertainment for the troops, September 1939.

60 A long queue outside a cinema, 1947.

Music. Shaw's *Pygmalion* was adapted and, as *My Fair Lady*, became a long-running musical.

These glittering shows attracted large audiences. Managers of other theatres tried to draw the crowds by putting on 'safe' plays. They revived the classical plays – by Shakespeare and Sheridan, for example – or they presented plays by well-known and popular playwrights. Christopher Fry followed the example of T S Eliot and wrote a number of verse dramas, in particular *The Lady's Not For Burning*. In the 1950s a new breed of playwrights came to the fore – and another new age began in the theatre.

The Angry Young Men

Samuel Beckett is an Irishman who has spent most of his life in Paris. In 1956, his play, *Waiting for Godot*, was directed by a then young Peter Hall, one of the new breed of post-war directors. Peter Hall himself admitted at the beginning of rehearsals: 'Haven't really the foggiest idea what some of it means, but if we stop and discuss every line we'll never open'. The two main characters in the play are tramps. They spend much of their time saying nothing, and when they do speak, as Peter Hall indicated, it is difficult if not impossible to decide what they are talking about. One impression left by the play is that many people lead utterly futile and wasteful lives in our modern, industralized society. When the play was first presented, many of the audience got up and walked out, shouting 'Disgrace!' 'Rubbish!' 'Disgusting!' But some critics praised the play and people flocked to see it – perhaps only to be baffled.

At the Royal Court Theatre in Sloane Square, the manager George Devine promised that he would allow young playwrights a chance to have their say. In the play *Look Back in Anger*, first presented at the Royal Court in 1956, John Osborne hit out at the British middle classes. As *The Times* critic said:

> The piece consists largely of angry tirades. The hero regards himself, and is clearly regarded by the author, as the specimen for the younger post-war generation which looks round at the world and finds nothing right with it.

Osborne and other young dramatists were expressing the anger of a generation which had been brought up to believe that, after the Second World War, Britain was a country in which class did not count, in which everyone had an equal opportunity to get on – but in which, in fact, there was still a great deal of class division and the rich still appeared to manipulate the less well-off.

Other playwrights wrote about the lives of ordinary people. A Salford schoolgirl, Shelagh Delaney, wrote *A Taste of Honey* (1958) – in which poor people from the slums of Salford are represented in their cheap lodgings. This and other plays were given the name 'kitchen-sink' drama, because they dealt with the ordinary, and often slightly sordid, real-life situations.

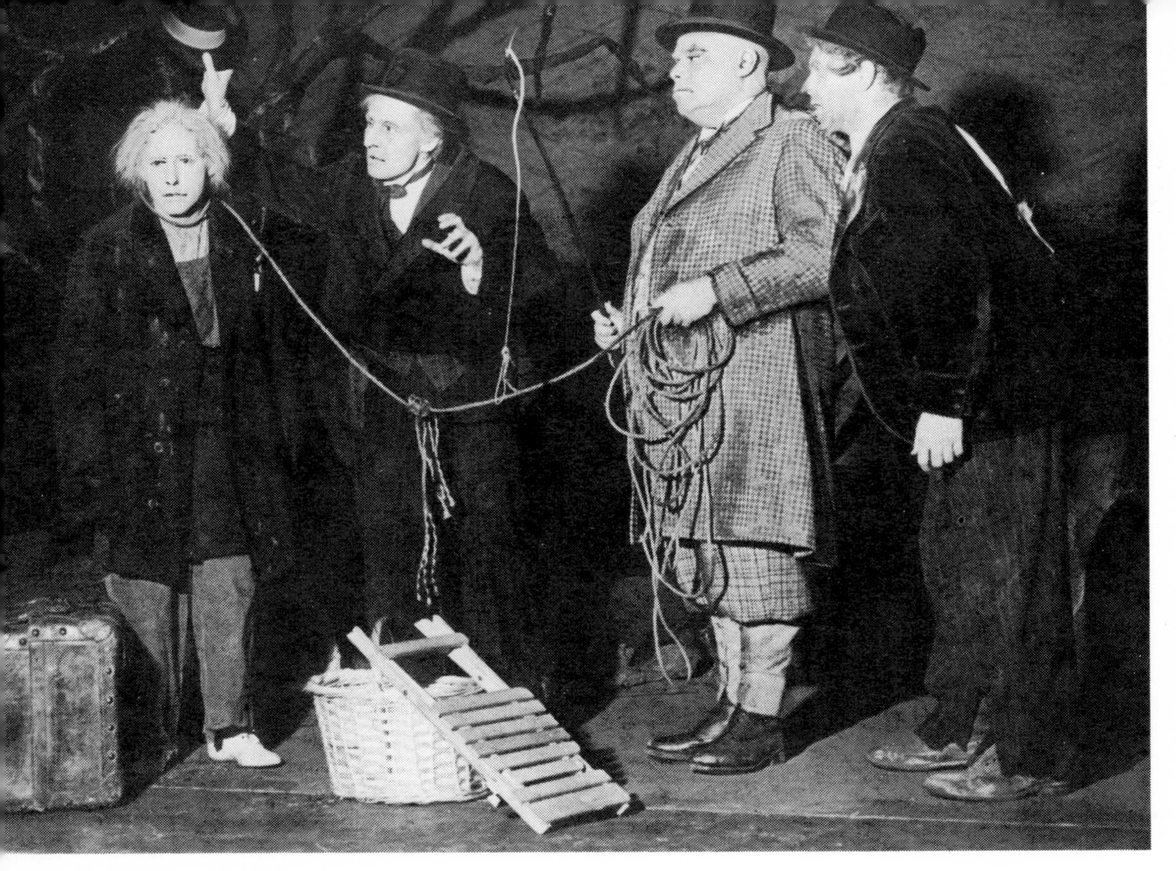

61 A scene from the original English production of Samuel Beckett's play *Waiting for Godot*, at the Arts Theatre, London, August 1955.

The new playwrights were often angry at the ways of the world; and their anger gained for them a reputation as 'the angry young men'. In his play *Roots* (1959), Arnold Wesker wrote:

> 'We know where the money lie,' they say, 'hell we do! The workers've got it, so let's give them what they want. If they want slop songs and film idols we'll give 'em that then. If they want words of one syllable, we'll give 'em that then. If they want the third rate, blust! we'll give 'em that then. Anything's good enough for them 'cos they don't ask for no more!' The whole stinkin' commercial world insults us and we don't care a damn.

But not all modern playwrights are concerned with the day-to-day lives of ordinary people. Terence Rattigan's *Ross* (1960), for example, discusses the strange life of Lawrence of Arabia; Robert Bolt's *A Man For All Seasons* (1960) is about Sir Thomas More and his struggle with Henry VIII. These plays, and especially their structure, owe much to the techniques of the cinema; indeed they have since been made into films.

62 A rehearsal at the Mermaid Theatre, London. The theatre was converted from an old warehouse. Notice the open stage and the bare brick walls.

Revival

In the 1950s and early 1960s, there was much pessimistic talk about the death of the living theatre, for which television was largely blamed. Today, however, we can see that such pessimism was unfounded. The theatre is as alive today as it ever was. True, many old theatres have been closed down and the buildings either demolished or adapted for some other purpose. But at the same time there has also been a great deal of theatre-building taking place. New theatres have been established in Nottingham, Leicester, Coventry, Guildford, Croydon, Leatherhead and many other towns. Under the Local Government Act of 1949, local councils were allowed to spend some of the revenue from rates on entertainment. Certain councils have used this money to help build and subsidize new theatres. Moreover, in 1964 the government appointed a Minister with special responsibility for the Arts, who was given a large sum of money to spend – over £20 million in 1970. The Arts Council which distributes this money has helped many local councils to build and run new theatres – and as a result there are now more theatres and more people going to watch live plays than there were in the 1920s and 1930s.

Stages and Scenery

The drama written in this century has been a mixture of escapism and social concern. The stages on which these and other plays are presented have also been a mixture – of old, glittering, realistic sets and new, stark scenery. Some theatres have revolving stages on which directors arrange multiple sets, so that the audience does not have to wait for a curtain to go down before switching from one scene to another. In other theatres ordinary stages also contain multiple sets, and each one is lit up as the need requires. In a few, including the Mermaid Theatre in London, there are open stages as there were in Shakespeare's time, and scenery plays a very minor part in a production. Others use the 'stage in the round' where the audience sit all around the stage and there is no scenery to help 'rouse the emotions of the viewers' – everybody's attention is focussed on the words.

Actors Today

Some actors belong to a theatrical company – such as the one which runs the National Theatre in London. Here a play is rehearsed and performed for several nights until everyone knows their part thoroughly. The play then passes into the repertoire of the company, which is able to perform it at almost any time it chooses for many years to come. Such companies are truly repertory companies.

An increasing number of plays are put on by theatre managers who pay a director and scene designer, and hire actors and stage hands, to put on a particular play which the manager thinks will do well. If enough people do not

63 *The Mousetrap* was first produced in 25 November 1952 and is now the longest running play of any kind in the history of the British theatre.

come to see it the producer loses money, dismisses his staff and the play is called off. But if the public likes the play, and is willing to come, then it may run for years – as Agatha Christie's *The Mousetrap* has done. This method of theatre management has many defects: if the play fails the actors and other staff are out of a job and their confidence suffers; if the play does well and runs for several years there is a danger that the actors will become stale. Whether the play does well or badly, money is wasted on sets and costumes which are specially produced for this play and this play alone, and which may never be used again because there is no company or organization built around the play. Even worse, perhaps, is that managers want only 'safe' plays which they think the public will flock to see. Too few managers are willing to risk their money on a play which might do well for a night or two, and which might therefore form part of the repertoire of an organized company, but has no attraction for the 'one-off' manager anxious to make a profit.

The number of young people anxious to get on to the stage continues to grow. Every year RADA and other training schools have more applicants than they have places. Each year young hopefuls join a local theatre company or work for one or other of the larger stock companies. They rehearse one play in the morning, while learning their lines for another play which will be performed a couple of weeks later. They receive relatively low wages and suffer frequent unemployment, but they still remain stage-struck – hoping no doubt that they, too, will one day enjoy the fame that has come to John Gielgud or Laurence Olivier, Peggy Ashcroft or Edith Evans.

These younger actors no longer see the cinema or television as a deadly rival to the live theatre. On the contrary, they see it as a source of income – for television and the cinema constantly need new material, and so need actors and actresses. Almost all the people who appear on films or television have come from drama schools and have learned their craft as members of one of the many theatrical companies.

Both cinema and television do many things very well. Great drama has been written for television, in which small casts intimately examine and work out problems under the eye of the camera, bringing us very close to the scene of the play as we sit comfortably in our living rooms. But we can never expect to share on television the intimate experience which we enjoy when we go to the live theatre, and take part with the actors and the rest of the audience in a live show. Only in the theatre can we get the human contact and living experience which, as the Greeks realized, was one of the essentials of theatre.

Further Reading

General Histories of the Theatre

Halliday, F E, *Cultural History of Britain,* Thames & Hudson, 1964
Mander, R and Mitchenson, J, *A Pictorial History of the English Theatre,* Hulton
Priestley, J B, *The Wonderful World of the Theatre,* Macdonald, 1969

Histories of the Periods and Topics Covered in this Book

Burton, H M, *Shakespeare and his Plays,* Longmans, Then and There Series
Chamberlin, E R, *Everyday Life in Renaissance Times,* Batsford, 1969
Hindley, Geoffrey, *The Medieval Establishment,* Wayland, 1970
Fox, Levi, *Shakespearean England,* Wayland, 1972
Laver, J R, *Victorian Vista,* Hulton, 1954
Laver, J R, *Edwardian Promenade,* Hulton, 1958
Mitchell, R J, *The Medieval Feast,* Longmans, Then and There Series
Murphy, E, *Pepys in London,* Longmans, Then and There Series
Priestley, J B, *The Edwardians,* Heinemann, 1970
Reader, W J, *Victorian England,* Batsford, 1974
Reeves, Marjorie, *The Medieval Feast,* Longmans Then and There Series
Seaman, L C B, *Life in Britain between the Wars,* Batsford, 1970
Sheppard, E J, *Ancient Athens,* Longmans, Then and There Series
Stewart, P, *Shakespeare and his Theatre,* Wayland, 1973
Taylor, Duncan, *Ancient Greece,* Methuen, 1957

Index

The numbers in **bold** refer to pages on which illustrations appear.